THIS VILLAGE IS CURSED

A 1940s Philip Bryce mystery

Peter Zander-Howell

Copyright © 2023 Peter Zander-Howell

All rights reserved.

Certain well-known historical persons are mentioned in this work. All other characters and events portrayed in this book are fictitious, and any similarity to real persons, alive or dead, is coincidental and not intended by the author. Real-world locations in this book may have been slightly altered.

No part of this book may be reproduced, or stored in a retrieval system, or transmitted in any form or by any means, electronic, mechanical, photocopying, recording, or otherwise, without the express permission of the publisher.

Cover photograph © 123rf

For Orson

PREFACE

A young provincial journalist receives a telephone call from a man who won't give his name. Anticipating the scoop of his career, Marcus Cunningham arranges to meet the informant at Liverpool Street station.

Subsequent events quickly draw in Scotland Yard detectives Chief Inspector Philip Bryce and his colleague Sergeant Alex Haig, as they conduct a complex murder investigation.

INTRODUCTION

DETECTIVE CHIEF INSPECTOR BRYCE

Philip Bryce is an unusual policeman. A Cambridge-educated barrister, he joined the Metropolitan Police in 1937 under Lord Trenchard's accelerated promotion scheme.

After distinguished army service in WW2, by 1949 he has become Scotland Yard's youngest Detective Chief Inspector.

His fiancée was killed during the war, but he recently married a woman whom he met on another murder case.

Bryce is something of a polymath, and has a number of outside interests – railways and cricket near the top of the list.

CONTENTS

Title Page
Copyright
Dedication
Preface
Introduction

CHAPTER 1	1
CHAPTER 2	40
CHAPTER 3	50
CHAPTER 4	61
CHAPTER 5	77
CHAPTER 6	97
CHAPTER 7	122
CHAPTER 8	136
CHAPTER 9	148
CHAPTER 10	167
CHAPTER 11	172
CHAPTER 12	188

CHAPTER 13	202
CHAPTER 14	217
CHAPTER 15	232
CHAPTER 16	239
CHAPTER 17	255
CHAPTER 18	262
Books In This Series	279

CHAPTER 1

Marcus Cunningham boarded the Norwich to London train when it made its 9:15 pm stop at Ipswich. Climbing into an empty third-class compartment in the rear carriage, he experienced the same degree of anticipation he had felt earlier that evening, when his meagre supper had been interrupted by the telephone bell.

Optimistic by nature, the young reporter was forever hopeful that, one day, he would learn something truly exceptional, and that this yet-to-happen event would become the big story which would establish him as a journalist. He had left his meal to answer the telephone, and was glad that he had done so. The anonymous caller claimed to be in possession of certain "*damning information*", of which both police and press "*must be made aware*".

Cunningham had listened with increasing excitement as the caller assured him that he would be provided with information, and documents of such significance they could not possibly be entrusted to the Royal Mail. The owner of the voice (and Cunningham had no idea who this could be) said he was prepared to hand over everything with two provisos. First: the reporter was to give no clue as to how he had come by the material when he contacted the police. Second: the documents must only be paraphrased to the police – under no circumstances were the originals to be handed over. Arrangements for their return would be made at the rendezvous – Liverpool Street station.

The caller continued setting out his conditions in the same meticulous manner, saying that although Cunningham would, of necessity, see his informant's face, he would not be given a name or any other details.

Cunningham was further warned that he would be closely watched. If there was the slightest suspicion that any observer – with or without a camera – had been sent to spy at Liverpool Street, the meeting would be aborted. A reporter on a rival newspaper would then become the recipient of the caller's "...*incendiary revelations...*".

The mysterious man made clear his assumption that the *Anglian Examiner,* in common with press convention, never revealed sources who wished to remain anonymous. If Cunningham should, at some later date, work out the informant's identity, he was to consider himself firmly bound by that protocol.

Although he had misgivings about this constraint, Cunningham didn't share them with his caller. The ethics of keeping his sources secret had never arisen in the context of the insipid stories he had so far published. Contributors to his copy were usually eager to be fully identified and, if possible, photographed alongside their champion heifer or 'best in show' vegetable marrow. But even so, the reporter knew that he would have no reservations about fulfilling the caller's anonymity condition in almost all circumstances.

The one possibility which caused him to have misgivings about the conditions was if, later that evening, he received information linked to a serious crime. The reporter felt that must surely fall beyond the bounds of the confidentiality pledge.

The incident which Cunningham had in mind was a murder, committed in his village four days before. Since the caller referred to information *"for the police"*, it seemed highly probable that he was to learn something related to that crime. He had been actively engaged in nosing around, talking to the detectives and parishioners in Ashton. He assumed that his involvement was known to the caller, and that was the reason why he had been approached.

Even allowing for the usual degree of telephonic distortion, the muffled words which reached Cunningham's ear convinced him that the man was attempting to disguise his voice. That subterfuge – along with the caller's insistence that he would never reveal his name – helped persuade Cunningham this was not a hoax. He thought it far more likely that a prankster would have readily given a false name and told other lies from the outset, rather than impose stipulations which might be rejected.

As the conversation progressed, Cunningham was certain that the informant really did possess incriminating knowledge but, for whatever reason, was reluctant to approach the police directly.

Was he an accomplice, perhaps, who wanted the assailant to be arrested, but without being dragged into an investigation himself? Had he seen, or discovered something, but was afraid that if he went to the police the killer would find out, and come looking for him? These, and several other thoughts, had passed through Cunningham's mind in the last few hours.

Travel arrangements to Liverpool Street had been issued, the caller specifying the train on which he should travel. He was also instructed to book himself a return ticket, because the meeting would take less than ten minutes and he could easily catch the eleven o'clock train back to Ipswich. He was to carry a copy of his own broadsheet newspaper, ensuring that the distinctive masthead was visible, and wait by the gate to Platform 6. This was where he would be met.

The reporter had much to think about as he replaced the telephone receiver and returned to his supper. Having agreed to all the caller's terms, by the time he had finished his pilchards on toast and drunk his cold tea, he had made a firm resolution. Irrespective of his acceptance of secrecy, he would give the police everything he possibly could about the man he was to meet, if he felt such action was justified.

Cunningham turned his head towards the compartment window. Heavy rain was beating against the glass, the little spots of water seeming to defy gravity as they streaked across the window in near horizontal lines. He amused himself for a while by watching the rain on the window, his mind wandering back to childhood and train journeys with his older brothers. Each boy would pick a globule of rain to 'race' across a compartment window, keeping score of their successes as they played. The first to reach five was declared overall winner of these droplet derbies.

He smiled to himself. It was a happy memory of his brothers, and a better one to dwell on than the dreadful fates which both had met in the war. It comforted him to know that their lives would be fully honoured in the family history he was writing in his spare time, and he spent the rest of his journey mentally reviewing everything he had so far assembled for this opus.

As the train passed Bethnal Green station, Cunningham stood up and began to ready himself. He fastened the buttons of his dark blue overcoat and took down his hat from the mesh luggage rack. Setting the grey homburg squarely atop his neatly combed brown hair, he checked his appearance in the mirror beneath the rack. A pleasant but very ordinary face looked back at him; inquisitive blue eyes its only – and very slight – claim to distinction.

Satisfied that he looked presentable, he lowered the window as the train stopped, and leaned out to operate the door handle. With his newspaper correctly arranged, he stepped down onto Platform 10, noticing that very few passengers were ahead of him. The train had been practically empty.

Cunningham was very familiar with Liverpool Street, having travelled in and out of it many times. He knew the station's unusual features, the most significant of these being that two of the platforms – all of which were well below street level – extended significantly further into the terminus than the others.

This oddity of layout came about when the station was built in separate parts. In the nineteenth century, the two main-line platforms at the eastern side of the station (serving the more distant destinations) were substantially longer than those serving the suburban lines. A few years later, when the station was extended further eastwards, the eight new platforms were also short. This meant that Platform 9 and Platform 10 – at which he had just alighted – divided the station to some extent.

Cunningham, and other passengers wishing

to pass at platform level from the new east side to the older west side (or vice versa), had to walk all the way around the ends of the three tracks which lay between these two protruding platforms. Anyone approaching the platforms at street level could bypass this detour, and use a footbridge instead, but that option wasn't available to him. His walk to Platform 6 would first take him along a narrow strip of the station concourse, bounded on one side by the rear wall of the Great Eastern Hotel and on the other by the tracks.

He proceeded down Platform 10 and turned right. As he walked towards the end of Platform 9 (where his return train would shortly arrive), a man stood facing him, only a few yards ahead. Dressed in a long black mackintosh and matching sou'wester, he had one hand tucked inside his coat and was clearly holding something out of sight.

Although Cunningham had been told to wait by Platform 6, he intuitively felt this was the man he was to meet, and that the mackintosh concealed the hand which held the promised evidence.

Hitching his newspaper a little higher in front of his chest, the reporter strode along, a sincere 'how-do-you-do?' smile on his lips in readiness for his first encounter with the informant.

Just as the gap between the two men narrowed to only a few feet, the approaching figure flung open his mackintosh. In one swift movement he brought out a sawn-off shotgun and discharged both barrels – almost simultaneously – into the reporter.

The impact threw the unsuspecting young man backwards. As he fell, he slipped over the platform edge and landed behind the buffers.

The gunman looked down at his target, then calmly turned and walked away. Ejecting the spent cartridges, he loaded fresh ones as he went, before once again concealing the weapon under his coat.

This shocking slaying took only seconds. Marcus Cunningham was given no warning. He had no chance of escape.

The brutal atrocity had, however, been witnessed from the footbridge. A uniformed army officer, walking slowly along the footbridge near the cafeteria, had been watching the late-night comings and goings on the concourse below as he waited for his own train. At the sound of the shotgun he started to run down the nearest flight of steps, drawing his pistol as he went. Arriving at platform level, he boldly confronted the gunman, who was now facing him.

"Hey you! Stop!"

The assassin stared back. For a fleeting instant he appeared to take notice. Then he moved to pull out his shotgun again.

The officer fired twice.

The gunman fell to the concourse floor, his weapon falling with him. He lay on his back, only the butt of the gun now visible beneath him.

The soldier moved forwards and dropped onto one knee. He quickly checked the assailant for signs of life at his neck and wrist, and found none. Replacing his pistol in its holster, he stood up and appeared to stagger a little, before starting the short walk back to the footbridge. He leaned heavily against the handrail for a moment to steady himself, before sitting down on a step.

Scant seconds later, a British Transport Commission police officer was running towards the spot, together with three British Railways staff. The four were met by two police constables. The City policemen had been scheduled to take a break from their respective beats, and happened to converge close to the Bishopsgate entrance to the train station as they made their way back to their base. Both had barely heard the shotgun blasts, and had attributed the sound to a car backfiring in the distance. As they neared the station they heard the soldier's two unmistakable pistol shots ring out. The policemen raced onto the footbridge, their whistles blaring as they ran.

Arriving at the bottom of the steps, the scene before them immediately explained the pistol shots. PC Edward Cowan bent over the slain gunman whilst PC Kenneth Foulger told the British Transport officer to take one of the railway men and round up all the travellers who were on the concourse at the time of the shooting. They were to be held together in a group, well away from the footbridge steps.

These were the people who had been sprinkled about the station only a few minutes before. Initially, they had been shocked and temporarily ossified by the unexpected gunfire. The first pair of shots had sounded like one, but the second pair were separate and clear. Crucially, however, the sound of all the shots had been distorted by the station's acoustics, making location of the danger difficult. Confused and frightened, passengers had flattened themselves onto the concourse floor, rather than run away. They were now moving again, but Foulger knew all must be detained for questioning.

Addressing the two remaining railway staff he said, "Your job is to make sure no new passengers arrive or leave the station via the Bishopsgate footbridge or the taxi drive."

With all this in hand, he turned to speak to the soldier, and a young woman who was standing nearby.

The army man explained what had happened in terse, jerky sentences, jabbing a condemnatory finger at the gunman as he spoke. "That fiend just mowed down a man!"

He jabbed again. "Mowed him down in cold blood. Sent him straight over the edge of Platform 9. Saw it all with my own eyes. Felt I had to do the necessary before the swine turned on anyone else."

He gave the back of his neck a hard rub and finished in a dazed voice, "Dashed if I can come to terms with what's happened!"

Quickly grasping that the two pistol shots heard outside in the street were not the only gunfire in the station that evening, Constable Foulger called to his colleague, still bent over the assailant and checking his pockets for identification.

"Eddie, take a gander at the end of Platform 9. Another body down there, apparently."

As the Constable was speaking, the young woman standing nearby moved closer to the footbridge and lowered herself onto the step beside the soldier. Elegantly dressed in a red coat with a turquoise angora beret and scarf, Foulger observed that she cut a rather lovely figure as she sat on the grubby step in the aftermath of the evening's vileness, the soft texture and vivid colour of her accessories contrasting charmingly with both the coat and her blonde hair.

Speaking clearly when questioned, she described what she had seen, and volunteered that the gunman had moved to use his weapon before the soldier had fired his own.

Constable Cowan returned. Having never seen the effects of a shotgun he was understandably sickened by the experience, but kept his feelings in check.

"Another body down there, right enough, Ken," he reported. "And no one's heard our whistles. We need back-up here – pronto. I'll leg it over the road and see who I can find." He ran up the steps, across the footbridge, and back into

Bishopsgate.

The British Transport officer and his railwayman assistant were managing to keep the majority of their charges to one side as instructed. A handful, however, possessed of a more intrusive and morbid curiosity, had broken away from their corral and were crowding around the end of Platform 9 to gawp at the gunman's victim.

Foulger barked sharply at them. "Oi! You lot! You do know this isn't a ruddy peepshow, don't you? Move away from there and show some respect!" He glowered at the voyeurs as they reluctantly obeyed his command and returned to the group.

When satisfied that his order had been obeyed, he carried on writing the details of the incident in his pocketbook, only looking up when his colleague returned, bringing reinforcements from Bishopsgate police station.

Sergeant Robert Layton briefly acknowledged his subordinate at the foot of the steps and confirmed that he was taking charge. Glancing around, he pointed to a convenient bench and told Foulger, "Shift these two over there, and watch them until I come back."

An assistant station master now arrived, and helpfully confirmed that there would be no more movement of trains at Platforms 9 and 10 until he was told otherwise. A quick conversation took place between the Sergeant and the railway official and a satisfactory compromise resulted.

The entire concourse between the two significant platforms, as well as the Bishopsgate footbridge and steps, were to be cordoned off. This, the two men agreed, was the best means of securing the scene for the police whilst allowing the rest of the station to function.

Satisfied with these arrangements, Sergeant Layton approached the group of travellers who had been on the concourse during the shootings and raised his voice to ask, "Is anyone here a witness? Did any one of you see anything of the first shooting, over there?"

All eyes automatically followed his finger, pointing towards the Platform 9 buffers. Shakes of the head and 'no', were the only responses.

"What about the second shooting? Anyone see anything of that?"

Again, heads obediently turned as directed and all gave the same responses as before – apart from one man. Dressed in the donkey jacket and flat cap of a Port of London stevedore, he piped up in a thick cockney accent:

"Them's 'oo you wants to talk to, guvnor. Jack'n'Jill on the bench ower there."

It was a casual but curiously apposite reference to the young couple. In their late twenties, both had blonde hair and uncommonly good looks. An attractive and smartly dressed pair, they could easily have been taken for siblings. When the docker had managed to locate the source of the pistol shots, he had spotted the armed soldier with the assassin at his feet, the girl in the red coat next closest to the scene. From this, he had correctly surmised that these two were the key witnesses.

This was not news to Sergeant Layton. When Constable Cowan had come barging through the doors of the police station looking for help, he had passed on what the docker was now saying. But Layton would have liked further corroboration of events. Allowing for the fact that the number of people using the station at that time of night was, inevitably, not great, he was nevertheless surprised that no one else had come forward from the assembled travellers and staff. Twenty years of experience had taught him that wherever there were fewer people at the scene of a crime, the resulting witnesses should, in theory, manage to see more, due to having a clearer line of sight.

Disappointed, but deciding there was nothing to be gained from the bystanders, he instructed that their identification should be checked and recorded, after which they could all leave.

Making his way back to the soldier and girl on the bench, the Sergeant's route took him past one of the station's long luggage barrows, broken and propped on its side against a wall. Something unusual about it caught his eye. He stopped and turned to face the wall for a better look, and quickly spied the anomaly which had attracted his attention: the toe of a brown leather boot was protruding from behind the barrow.

Apprehensive, and mindful that he might discover another gunman, Layton slowly moved forwards to investigate, truncheon in hand. As he drew closer he realised he would have no need of his baton and replaced it on his belt.

Tugging up his trouser knees, he sank onto his haunches by the wall and found himself facing a diminutive woman, tightly compressed into the prism of space behind the slope of the barrow. She wore a nondescript brown coat and a brown felt hat, the brim of which was squashed down on both sides of her head, wedged as she was between the wall and the bed of the barrow. The effect resembled a spaniel's drooping ears about her pinched and sad little face.

Crouched with her shoulders hunched into the upturned collar of her overcoat, a small overnight bag clasped against her legs, the tiny woman looked quite pitiful as she did her best to become invisible. Very much alive inside her makeshift hide, she was also very much afraid.

Layton spoke slowly and kindly, "Am I right in thinking you've seen something that's upset you, madam? Something near Platform 9, perhaps?"

Unhappy nodding gave him the answer he expected.

"Ahhh, you're not alone then. Other people have also had a nasty experience tonight. The police are in charge, and there's no longer any danger. I must ask you to come with me and help with our enquiries."

More unhappy nodding reassured the Sergeant that the woman was not so traumatised she couldn't understand what he was saying. He took the handles of her little grip and stood up. Pulling the top edge of the heavy wooden barrow bed away from the wall, he allowed his mute new witness the dignity of standing to emerge, rather than crawling out as she had crawled in.

With the woman now in full view, he could see that she was in early middle age, and no more than four feet nine inches tall. One of her woollen stockings was torn and bloodied, and he felt a surge of sympathy and protectiveness towards her, exactly as he would have done for an injured and frightened child in the same situation. Stooping forwards, he adjusted his height to hers as far as he was able, drew one of her arms through his own, and slowly led her to the bench, where he guided her to take a seat beside the younger woman.

"I've heard what happened here, sir," said Layton to the army officer, "and I appreciate what you've done. But I must ask you to hand over your pistol. Routine, that is."

"Yes, of course, Sergeant, I understand." The soldier's voice was now steadier and more controlled. He took the holstered pistol off his belt and held it out to the policeman. "Safety's on, and it's still loaded."

As Layton reached out to accept the weapon the soldier hesitated and retracted his hand a little, anxiety sweeping over his handsome face. "You will take good care of it won't you?" he asked, "I'm responsible to the army for it."

"No need to worry yourself on that score, sir."

"You'll want a statement from me, I suppose? I don't know if anyone else saw the first man get shot, but I certainly did. Not what I expected in Liverpool Street tonight!"

"That's correct, sir, we will need your statement," agreed Layton. He looked at the two women, "You as well, ladies; we'll need a statement from both of you. Trouble is – and I'll give you all fair warning – at this time of night we don't have many officers on duty.

"Right now, there are no detectives at all in the station. So I'm afraid it will be some time before you get to wherever it was you were going."

Tired acceptance from the three witnesses met this unwelcome news.

"If you wouldn't mind waiting here for just a little longer, there are a few more things I need to attend to. Then we can go to the police station, and at least get you all some refreshment and make you a bit more comfortable while you wait."

Sergeant Layton was true to his word. Having issued further instructions to his constables and the British Transport officer, he returned ten minutes later to escort his witnesses up the stairs to Bishopgate, and across the road.

***

It was over an hour before the promised help materialised. Detective Inspector Richard Playford, having already turned in for the night, quickly dressed and made his way to Liverpool Street station. With recruitment and retention problems resulting in a regular increase to his workload, the DI had already put in a good whack of overtime that day. However, when his telephone bell rang and duty once again called, he immediately prepared to meet it. He first issued a few orders to the officer who had summoned him, and then invigorated his tired mind and body with some coffee before leaving home.

Arriving in the railway station, Playford found the Police Surgeon already crouching on the tracks beside the buffers at the end of Platform 9. "Hello John," he called down to the crown of the medic's black trilby.

Doctor McNally looked up. "'Evening Dick – or 'morning, I suppose would be more accurate," he replied. "I must say, it's a long time since you and I were called out on such a filthy night, and when we are, the death usually turns out to be either accident or suicide. Not this time, though!"

McNally was right about the weather. Sleet had started to fall with the hammering rain, and a strong wind was adding its force to that already bitterly cold combination. A penetrating draught could be felt even under the great roof of the train shed.

"Not much I can tell you at the moment, except that this chap died from shotgun wounds. Must have been from very close range. I think two shots, and the spread is minimal. I'll do a pellet count at the *post mortem*.

"You probably have several witnesses and know the time of death already, Dick, but two hours ago at the very most, for this one.

"There's some stuff in the pockets; damaged by the blast, inevitably. Do you want to come down and take a look, or wait until I get him to the morgue?"

"I'll come down and do his pockets," said Playford. "Have to find out who he is as soon as possible. The gunman too; need to know who he is." The DI sat on the edge of the platform and lowered himself onto the tracks beside the doctor.

"I've looked at the other one already," said McNally as the DI joined him. "Two shots into the heart from the front. Probably from a point three eight handgun. Again, I'll confirm after the PM, but your officers tell me they have the pistol used, so there won't be much news for you there, either."

McNally moved aside to allow the detective to take his place. "One of the constables has already done a search of the man on the concourse. Apart from eight twelve-bore cartridges in his pockets, nothing else on him at all. They've also picked up two empty cartridges, presumably ejected after this man was shot. Professional assassin, if you ask me."

Playford thanked the surgeon and turned his attention to the slain reporter. Close up, and now lying on his back to where the Doctor had rolled him, Cunningham presented a dreadful sight. Gritting his teeth, and glad that the onset of winter meant he was wearing leather gloves, the DI set about removing some clinging tatters of crimson-coloured newspaper. He started to feel in pockets, leaving the most damaged, inner breast pocket, until last.

To the constable standing guard on the platform, Playford called: "Make a note, Jenkins. Some coins in trousers. Return part of a train ticket in jacket ticket pocket. Notepad and two pencils in coat pocket."

A minute later he continued: "Overcoat inner pocket has damaged wallet, containing some pound and ten-shilling notes. Soaked handkerchief in outer coat pocket.

"ID card in the side pocket of jacket."

Playford, distasteful as he found the task, opened this document. Rubbing his gloved fingertip across the card he was astonished to be able to piece together the name. "Marcus Cunningham," he said, "from somewhere in either Suffolk or Norfolk – I can't make out the first letters of the county because they've been shot through, and the rest of the address isn't clear either.

"Three keys on a ring; one is car ignition."

He felt around some more before concluding, "That's the lot as far as I can tell, Jenkins." He pushed everything into one of the large, reinforced envelopes he always carried with him, then stood up and addressed the constable again, "Grab a fire bucket of sand for me would you, so I can get this off my gloves."

Jenkins speedily obliged.

Somewhat cleaned up, Playford told the surgeon, "That's my bit done, as best as I can do it, John; but it'd be a help if you take another look through his pockets later, and let me know if I've missed anything.

"And you can arrange to get them both off to the morgue whenever you like. Probably take an hour or so before that happens, so I'll try to find someone to take pictures and fingerprints before they go. Don't you wait on that though – if you can get them away sooner, so much the better. Clearing the station must be a priority."

The DI clambered back onto the platform and gave another instruction to the officer on guard, "Carry on here, Jenkins, until he's taken away."

Seeing McNally fastening his medical bag, Playford offered a hand to the police surgeon and helped him off the tracks. The pair walked to where the gunman still lay on top of his weapon.

"Assuming he reloaded that thing, I reckon we can count ourselves lucky that it didn't discharge again when he fell – killing or maiming who knows how many others into the bargain. We'd have had even more to do tonight, John," observed the Inspector.

Dr McNally laughed. "Always a silver lining for you in everything, Dick, no matter how dire the circumstances."

The DI guffawed, and removed a glove to exchange a friendly goodbye handshake.

Addressing PC Cowan, who was standing guard over the gunman, he said, "We're short of CID men tonight, so scrounge a bit of sacking from somewhere, Constable, and bring that shotgun back to the station. Do you know how to break it and eject any cartridges?"

Cowan looked doubtful. "Is it similar to breaking a revolver, sir?"

"Near enough. The shooter's wearing gloves, but even so, don't touch the barrel or butt with your bare fingers. Take it to my room with any cartridges." To the remaining Constable he said, "Foulger, you can take over from Cowan until the gunman's taken away."

Satisfied that he had seen and done as much as possible, Playford climbed the steps onto the footbridge, and exited the station into Bishopsgate. The road was practically deserted at that hour in the morning, with only a couple of vehicles proceeding cautiously through the driving slush. With his coat collar up and his hat brim down, he turned to face the police station and took the shortest path by crossing the road diagonally (not something he could ever do when the road was busy), and was inside the police station within a minute.

"Any luck in getting me someone in CID?" he asked the Desk Sergeant as he removed his coat and shook the precipitation from it.

"Yes, sir; I got hold of DS Phillips – he should be here soon. I also spoke to the Superintendent at home, as you instructed. He said you should carry on.

"The three witnesses are all in separate interview rooms. They've had refreshments, and the lady who hurt herself has been attended to."

The DI grunted.

"Oh, and Bob Layton put the soldier's pistol on your table, sir," added the Sergeant.

The stimulating effects of Playford's coffee were wearing off, just as the exhaustion of an over-long working day was asserting itself. He wearily signalled his thanks and slowly tramped up the stairs to his office.

Emptying the contents of the envelopes onto the side table which held the holstered pistol, he sat down at his desk and closed his eyes. At times like this he found that even a few minutes' quiet, snatched here and there, were beneficial.

Cowan's arrival with the shrouded shotgun ended his brief respite.

"On there, with the pistol and the rest," instructed Playford.

As the Constable left the room he held the door open for another arrival.

"Glad you were available, Phillips," said the Inspector to the Detective Sergeant. "Bad enough that we're perennially short of CID officers anyway, and in the middle of the night as well…"

Phillips was by nature a slow-moving and slow-thinking individual, even when well-rested and fresh at the start of a working day. He would never normally be Playford's first choice of assistant – especially not in the middle of the night – but the Inspector was pleased to see him, nonetheless.

"I was already asleep, sir," was Phillips' reproachful comment.

"Likewise!" responded the DI crisply. "But we knew getting dragged out of bed is part of the job, and we shouldn't have signed up if we couldn't take the joke. Anyway, you've presumably heard the outline: one man murdered with a sawn-off shotgun, and the shooter killed by a soldier using his army-issue sidearm.

"Everyone who saw anything is waiting for us downstairs, but the first thing we need to do is find out what we can about the dead men.

"I've only just got back myself, and the bodies were still at Liverpool Street when I left. Get yourself a camera and a bag, Phillips, and nip over there sharpish. I want the usual facial shots. Prints off both men, too; we'll ask the Yard if they can match them.

"When you're done at the station, drop the film off and make sure it's marked urgent. No one around to do anything about it tonight, of course, but we need it developed and printed as fast as possible tomorrow. Once the photographs are distributed we'll see if anyone recognises the shotgun merchant.

"That shouldn't take you above fifteen or twenty minutes. As soon as you've done, come back here and look at this little lot," Playford pointed at the contents of his envelope. "There was nothing on the assassin apart from extra ammunition, but the personal effects of the first victim are all in that pile. There's an ID card, but apart from the name – Marcus Cunningham – hard to read because of the pellet holes and blood. Clean it up and do your best to piece together everything you can about who he was and where he came from.

Playford rubbed his face with both hands and hauled himself out of his chair. "I'm going down to speak to the witnesses. Come and find me when you've worked out as much as you can about Mr Cunningham."

Making his way downstairs and into the nearest interview room, the DI introduced himself to the poorly dressed little lady, noticing that a fresh bandage was showing through her torn stocking.

"I'm sorry you found yourself involved in all this unpleasantness, madam, and that you were injured into the bargain," he began. "Take your time and tell me who you are, and everything you saw from when you got off the train."

Tense and drawn, Mildred Cooper complied with the instruction, managing to speak coherently and in a surprisingly strong voice. She gave her name and an address in Bergh Apton, Norfolk, where she lived with her husband and mother-in-law.

"I got off the Norwich train," she said. "I was in the 'Ladies Only' compartment in one of the middle coaches. There weren't many passengers, and by the time we came towards the end of the platform, the others were well ahead of me.

"That poor young man..." she faltered "...he was behind me to begin with. I thought he was on my train, but I suppose he could have been coming from another platform. Anyway, I don't walk very fast, so I noticed him first when he passed me after I got off the train."

"Was he carrying anything apart from a newspaper?"

Mrs Cooper shook her head. "I don't think so. No valise or umbrella; just the paper."

She continued, "I'm going to stay with my sister in Peckham – that's where I'm from – so I had to get across to the underground. I made that right turn at the end of Platform 10, and so did the man in front of me. Perhaps he was going to the tube as well."

She paused and pressed trembling fingers

against her lips.

Playford watched, and wondered if Mildred Cooper was about to crack under the strain of recalling what she had seen. She wouldn't be the first witness to do that in front of him, and he wouldn't have blamed her if she did. He was pleased when a deep and steadying intake of breath preceded the resumption of her evidence.

"Anyways, as I turned the corner he was a few yards in front of me, as close to the rails as you can get. That's when I saw a man beside the wall of the big hotel, coming towards us."

The words were hardly out of her mouth when she reconsidered. "Or he may have been standing still. I can't say for sure. I know I saw him well enough, but I wasn't really looking at him at that point – only sort of *noticing* that he was there, as you do.

"Suddenly, there was a loud bang-bang. The man in front of me...he seemed to lift up and fly over the platform edge.

"I couldn't move for a second. But I could see the man with the gun ever so clear, because with the young man..." she ground to a halt, and breathed deeply again; "...with the young man gone, there was no one between the gunman and me.

"He didn't look my way; he was looking down onto the lines. But I thought if he did look up he'd see me for sure. Then he'd want to shoot me too, because I'd seen him and what he did."

Mrs Cooper faltered once more, before rallying and concluding her recollections. "That's when I ran away and hid. The Sergeant found me and brought me here. I'm still ever so scared."

Playford wasn't so tired that he missed the catch in her voice and the shimmer of the tears accumulating in her eyes. He thought she had suppressed her emotions admirably, but realised that an element of delayed shock might soon overtake her. He did his best to calm her.

"Now, now; don't you go on being afraid, Mrs Cooper, there's really no need for that. The gunman won't be coming after you or anyone else; he was killed by a soldier almost immediately."

She nodded. "Yes. Yes, I knew there was more shooting, although the second bangs sounded different."

Apart from asking whether the gunman or his victim had said anything to one another, to which she replied they had not, or at least, not that she heard, Playford could think of no further questions.

"Thank you, Mrs Cooper, what you've said has been very clear. I'll get someone to take your statement, and when that's done you can go on to your sister's. I'll arrange for a police officer to take you there by car."

Playford left the first interview room to move to the next.

The Inspector found his second witness waiting with an air of expectation. Brenda

Edwards' responses to the DI's questions were concise and given briskly. She had dined with her godmother in Islington, then travelled by tube from Angel to Moorgate, before walking the short distance to Liverpool Street to take a train home.

While standing by the gate to Platform 8 she heard the sound of the shotgun. She had turned too slowly to see anything of that first shooting; but had seen the gunman reloading his weapon and hiding it under his coat as he walked in her general direction.

That was when she first became aware of the soldier bounding down the last of the footbridge steps. When he reached the bottom she realised he was holding a pistol. He had faced the gunman and yelled at him. She had definitely heard him cry out 'stop'.

Miss Edwards looked past Playford's shoulder into the distance as she retrieved her memories; then turned her gaze on the detective again.

"For a second, Inspector, I thought the gunman was going to obey the command. But then he pulled his coat aside and started bringing up his gun towards the soldier. That's when the soldier fired two shots. I saw all of that from start to finish."

The girl described how, after witnessing the second shooting, she had sat with the young army man on the steps until they were moved to a bench. She had chatted to him about her own war experience.

"I was an Auxiliary Territorial Service officer during the war, operating heavy anti-aircraft guns in a mixed Royal Artillery battery. Loud bangs don't frighten me."

Playford found that easy enough to believe. Brenda Edwards was extremely self-assured, and he felt that despite her youthfulness – she looked no more than twenty-seven or eight – she would have been a capable pair of hands in war time. Nor did he find it inconsistent when she added:

"It wouldn't be true, though, if I told you I wasn't upset by what I saw tonight, Inspector. I felt quite winded soon after." She tapped the rim of her empty mug with a scarlet-polished fingertip, "But someone here knows how to make a decent cup of tea; so I'm much more myself now."

Satisfied that he had another credible witness, Playford thanked Miss Edwards and asked her to wait until his Sergeant arrived to take down her statement. Wishing the girl 'goodnight', he made his final move along the corridor. As he was about to enter the third room, Sergeant Phillips appeared.

"Marcus Cunningham, sir, lived at sixty-something – I couldn't make out the second digit – Fonnereau Road, if I've got that right. Funny name. That's definitely in Suffolk and not Norfolk, because I could make out the 'S' near enough; but the name of the town was shot right through. I'm thinking he might have been a journalist, sir. The notebook is full of squiggles."

The DI frowned, deep vertical lines filling the narrow gap between his eyebrows. "A reporter, eh? And from Suffolk? Well away from his own patch then, that's for sure."

He tipped his head to one side and regarded his Sergeant thoughtfully. "I'd be wondering about the reason for that, Phillips – him being in London with the tools of his trade in his pocket – even if I hadn't read there'd been a shotgun murder in Suffolk a few days ago."

Playford leaned back against the corridor wall and allowed the structure to support his tired body a little. "I'll get on to the locals at sun-up," he said. "Not much point trying in the middle of the night. If the cases are linked, I'm thinking they'll take the lead role in all this. Or, even more likely, the City and Suffolk will agree between them to hand everything over to the Yard.

"You get yourself in there, Sergeant," he said, pointing at the first interview room door, "and take Mrs Cooper's statement. Basically, she witnessed Mr Cunningham's shooting. Be extra nice to her; what she saw was upsetting, to put it mildly.

"When everything's signed, find a car and someone to take her to her sister's in Peckham."

Phillips looked askance at this.

"Yes, I know it's way outside our patch," Playford held up a warning forefinger, "and tell whoever it is to make sure they see her safely all the way in. After what she's gone through tonight, I don't want to hear she was left hanging about outside.

"Then you can move next door, and take the young lady's statement. Time you've done those two, I'll have finished with the soldier, and you can have him."

Sergeant Phillips acknowledged his instructions, and went to introduce himself to Mrs Cooper as Playford let himself into the adjoining room.

Unlike the women, who had both been anticipating their interview, the DI found the soldier slumped back in his chair, legs elevated and eyes closed. His boots were on the floor and his feet were on the small table alongside his army cap and untouched tea. Hearing the door shut, he stood up groggily and started to pull his boots back on, apologising as he did so. He spoke in a deep voice with an 'Oxford' accent:

"Do pardon my trotters on your table. I felt an overwhelming need to stretch out and shut down for a bit – and the floor didn't look overly comfortable!"

Playford, experienced and understanding of the various ways people behaved following a dangerous encounter, offered his own apology. "Yes, well I'm sorry to have kept you, Lieutenant."

He introduced himself and made a request to the soldier which hadn't been necessary for the two women. "You've the most to tell me, sir, so not too fast, please. I haven't got anyone to take notes tonight, and I can only write in longhand.

"First, your name and address, if you would; and why you were in Liverpool Street tonight."

"Reginald Johnson, Royal Norfolk Regiment, currently based at Colchester. It won't take me long to tell you what happened, Inspector, because the whole thing only took about a minute from start to finish."

Playford overlooked the curse. It was at the mildest end of what he'd heard in nearly thirty years as a policeman, and didn't alter his first impression of the young soldier as a fine specimen of His Majesty's officer class. Tall, clear-eyed, well-spoken and well turned-out, Johnson easily fulfilled the description 'clean-cut' in every way.

"I'd been out on the town with a couple of friends. All very staid, mind you – just a meal and a show. I came into Liverpool Street from Bishopsgate, to take the train back to the barracks. I had some time to spare, so I was watching the world go by from the footbridge."

The young army officer began to give his recollections in clear segments, pausing between each, evidently reliving them one by one.

"I was just meandering along the bridge and happened to be looking towards the hotel – my train would be leaving from Platform 9, but it hadn't yet arrived. If it had been standing there already I wouldn't have had the clear view of the area at the end of those two long platforms that

I did. I saw this man suddenly open his coat and bring out a sawn-off shotgun. For a second, I couldn't believe my eyes. It didn't take much longer than that for him to fire both barrels. I saw his target swept off his feet and onto the track. Absolutely no hope for him.

"I think I may have been running before the sound of the blasts had even cleared the air. I know I went barrelling hell-for-leather down the steps."

Johnson blinked rapidly and shook his head. "Looking back, I can't believe I didn't go base-over-apex, I was going at such a crazy lick.

"I had my pistol in my hand at the bottom – but I've absolutely no memory of releasing it from the holster and pulling back the slide. Pure instinct, I suppose.

"By that time, the madman had turned and was nearing Platform 8. I shouted at him; 'stop you' or 'you stop' – something of that sort. But he opened his coat and was bringing the gun out again. So I shot him. Twice. Then he was on the ground."

Johnson lowered his head into his hands and drove his fingers deep into his hair, leaving it tousled and his appearance less neat. Playford could see that the Lieutenant was not unaffected by what had happened.

"I may be in the army, Inspector, but I've never actually shot anyone at close quarters before," confided the soldier. "I'm not ashamed to admit it's fairly rattled me up.

"Anyway, I went and sat at the bottom of the steps, and that nice girl in the red coat joined me. Seems she saw everything. Later, she told me she'd been in the ATS and talked about her work during the war. I think she was trying to take my mind off matters – awfully sweet of her, really." Johnson looked embarrassed. "I reckon she's had more gun battle experience than I have!"

He sat back and shrugged his shoulders. "That's it. That's all I can tell you, Inspector. Everything I saw. Everything I did."

Playford wrote silently.

"This is all a bit complicated," he said after a while, recapping his fountain pen and clipping it back inside the breast pocket of his jacket.

"You can probably appreciate that a sawn-off shotgun is a weapon used only by the worst and most violent sort of criminal – and rarely even then, thankfully." He gave a sigh and a mirthless little laugh. "But never you mind about all that, Lieutenant; it's something for me and my team to get to the bottom of.

"The good news for you is that there's no doubt a coroner's jury will bring in a verdict of justifiable homicide for what you did tonight.

"Looking over what everyone has told me, it's probably the best thing that could have happened – you've prevented him killing anyone else."

A genuine smile now flitted across Playford's weary face. "Shouldn't wonder if you aren't fêted for a hero, Lieutenant, once the papers get hold of the story. Maybe even a bravery award coming your way. I say that because it's more than likely that the same gunman was involved in another recent murder. I doubt I'll be proved wrong if I tell you that this has all the hallmarks of a gangland killing."

Johnson's eyes widened in horror as the Inspector spoke. "Good God!" he exclaimed.

Despite Playford's well-meant words about justifiable homicide, the Lieutenant was now looking extremely worried. The suggestion of organised criminals was highly disconcerting to the army man, and he said so.

"Might not such characters want retribution for what I did to their henchman? I hope you can see why I won't be at all keen to see my part in all this splashed across the papers – this assassin may have friends who will want to come and, er, have a little chat with me!"

Johnson rubbed his scalp again. "I don't think the army would be too happy, either, if his cronies manage to find me and take a pop at me, just because my name and picture was in all the dailies."

Playford gave a sombre nod. "Yes, I do see that. Well, we can certainly keep your name away from the press and public for the time being, sir. But you'll have to give evidence at both inquests – there's no getting around that. And when that happens, it'll be up to the coroner how he deals with it all on the day."

Johnson looked far from mollified.

Playford saw this and did his best to ease the soldier's mind. "There are ways and means in these situations, sir; ways and means.

"For starters, the police, or you, or perhaps the War Office even, could make an application for you to be allowed to write your name and address down, rather than say them out loud. I'm sure such a request would be viewed favourably, in the circumstances. But we can think about all that later, and decide nearer the time."

"Thank you." Johnson finally sounded placated. "There's another thing, though. I'm being demobbed in three days' time. I was intending to go straight back to my parents' home in Wiltshire. But one of the friends I met tonight has fixed me up with an interview with Peterson and Harris here in the City. He works there, and says I'm a shoo-in for a job. So it looks as though I'll be staying in London after all. I'll let you have an address within a day or so.

"But before we get to the inquest stage, Inspector, one of your chaps made me hand over my pistol earlier." The Lieutenant quickly squashed any suggestion of criticism of Sergeant Layton's action, "Completely correct of him, I know. But it's service property, after all, and part of my uniform.

"Since it isn't in dispute that it was my pistol which killed the gunman; and given that you accept my reaction was lawful in the face of extreme threat, might I have it back?"

Playford pondered this. Serious consideration had to be given to the possibility that Johnson's name, despite every effort to keep it secret, could somehow find its way onto a criminal hit list. It hardly seemed right to deprive the soldier of the weapon which had, by all accounts, already saved his own life – and maybe an unknown number of other lives on Liverpool Street station. Not to mention how many more lives the soldier may have saved from future assassinations elsewhere, if the gunman really was a hired professional.

"Yes," he agreed at last. "I don't see why not. My Sergeant will come and take your formal statement in a while. Once you've signed that, you'll be free to go. I'll fetch your gun for you now."

Playford returned to his office. Grumbling to himself once more about the state of his side table, he removed Johnson's pistol and took it downstairs. Sergeant Phillips was saying goodbye to Miss Edwards as he approached.

"Do you think the Lieutenant will be in trouble for what he did, Inspector?" asked the young woman as she pulled on a pair of gloves.

"No, Miss, he won't be." Playford held up the holstered pistol. "I'm just about to give his gun back before he leaves. Thank you again for your help tonight, and we shall no doubt meet again at the inquest. Can you get home all right?"

"Oh yes, you needn't trouble about me; I'll take a taxi. Good night to you both."

Playford thought the cab fare to Chingford at that time of night wouldn't be cheap, but he correctly suspected this would not be a problem. Miss Edwards had the look of someone who 'came from money'.

"Right, Phillips," he said as the girl moved out of earshot, "I'm leaving as soon as I've given Johnson his gun.

"When you've taken his statement, you do the same. I'll see you back here later in the morning, when we've both had a bit of kip."

CHAPTER 2

At his home in Leyton, the DI dragged himself unwillingly out of bed a little after seven o'clock. Declining his wife's offer of breakfast, he responded to her anxious look with a reassurance that he would get something in a café near the police station, later. By half past seven he was on a Central Line train into Liverpool Street.

As soon as he entered his office he saw that the carnage on his side table looked even worse in daylight than it had in artificial light earlier that morning, the red stains having become more brownish. "Why on earth didn't I dump everything on the floor instead of the table?" he chided himself. Had he taken time to answer his own question his response would have been both simple and obvious; decisions taken when almost exhausted tend not to be the best decisions.

Seated at his desk, he picked up the three signed witness statements his Sergeant had left for him. As he began reading these, Phillips knocked and entered.

"Ah, the very man I want to speak to. Have

we heard from Dr McNally if there was anything else of interest on Mr Cunningham when he got him to the mortuary?" he asked. "Something I might have missed – a photograph of a wife or sweetheart, for example?"

"Nothing, sir. Only what you found yourself and is on the table here. Phillips pointed at each item as he spoke. "ID. Wallet with three pounds in notes; three and fourpence in change. Return ticket to Ipswich. Hanky. Three keys. The notebook and pencils."

"Ah yes, the notebook."

Playford joined his colleague at the side table to take another look at the reporter's pad. It had escaped the pellet shot, but had dried blood on its cardboard covers. Flicking both covers open, he saw there was nothing written on the reverse of either. He immediately ripped them off, and put them with the other items on the table.

"I'm not destroying evidence here, but I don't see why anyone should be needlessly upset by handling the book with those on."

He tapped the now exposed pages of the pad. "When you go downstairs, have a look and see who we've got in the station today to decipher this little lot and type it all up."

Phillips shook his head. "Done that already, sir. I've still got some notes on that Eastcheap case that need typing, so I took them into Clerical before I came up. Influenza's ripped through the office. Just one copy typist showed up today, and she's full of the sniffles."

"In that case we'll need help from a secretarial agency. Get them to send someone over. I've heard there are at least two languages – if that's the right word – Pitman's and Gregg's. Since we don't know which has been used, a secretary with both would be best, if there is such a person. Anyway, I want someone here as soon as possible.

"That's all for you at the moment, Phillips. I'm going upstairs to brief the Super, and then I'll give Ipswich a bell. I've a feeling that this won't be our case for much longer."

"Well I won't weep if that's the way things go, sir," said Phillips laconically as the two detectives made their way into the corridor.

The DI found his boss and briefed him on the night's events. As soon as the possible link with the Suffolk case was mentioned, the Super said that he would consult the Commissioner.

Playford returned to his desk. It was a little after eight-thirty when he placed his call to the East Suffolk Force. A connection was very quickly made and he was put through to Detective Inspector Catchpole, who confirmed that he was in charge of the investigation into the Suffolk shooting.

Playford outlined what had happened in Liverpool Street the previous evening.

"Strewth!" exclaimed Catchpole. He had listened without comment as his opposite number described the station shootings, but interrupted the City detective as soon as he heard Marcus Cunningham's name. Supplying a fortuitous piece of crucial information to the London DI he said, "I've met him, and I know where he lives in Ashton! He was following the murder case there, and pestered me for a statement a couple of times. It looks as if his digging around might have been a major problem for someone.

"I'll have to take this straight up to my Superintendent, Playford," he continued. "Given the City connection and a possible professional assassin, I'm pretty sure he'll take it to our Chief. Then, pound to a penny, the Yard will be called in."

Playford laughed. "I'm with you on that. I wouldn't mind betting that my Commissioner will be ringing your Chief Constable in next to no time. I don't expect to be responsible at this end for much longer."

The call was concluded just as Sergeant Phillips poked his head around the door to report that a shorthand typist was on her way.

"Good. Find someone to clear that side table top, Phillips. She can sit there when it's cleaned up."

The internal telephone rang. As Playford picked up the handset, he motioned that his Sergeant could go.

"We're summoned to HQ," said the Superintendent at the other end of the line. "The Commissioner wants to discuss the shootings. I'll meet you downstairs in five minutes and we'll take

Shanks's pony."

London's City – the 'square mile' – had always had a separate constabulary, despite being completely surrounded by the enormous area covered by the Metropolitan police force. There had been talk of merging responsibility in 1839, soon after the Met had been formed, but the influential City had seen off that suggestion. There had been more talks over the next hundred years, but they had been similarly inconclusive, and nothing had changed. Ultimate responsibility for the City constabulary still rested with the Common Council in the Guildhall.

Apart from Bishopsgate, the City now had only one other police station available to the public – Cloak Lane, which was also situated close to a major railway terminus, Cannon Street. A third police station, in Moor Lane, had been destroyed in the Blitz. The two policemen were now making their way to the headquarters, not – as might be expected – in the Guildhall, but located some two hundred yards away in Old Jewry .

The two officers walked down Old Broad Street towards Bank, appreciating that the temperature had risen a little from the previous night, with the clouds clearing just enough to allow an occasional feeble ray of sunshine to reach the pavement. The Superintendent mentioned the case only once – to declaim his views on the evil of sawn-off shotguns. The conversation then reverted to a fraud matter which was occupying a good proportion of the City's small detective force.

On arrival at the City constabulary's headquarters, the two men were told to take a seat. Both expected to be kept waiting for a long time, and were surprised when a woman in civilian clothes approached them not two minutes later.

"Sir Hugh will see you now, gentlemen," said the secretary.

Playford, who rarely visited headquarters, had never been in the Commissioner's office before and had only spoken to him half a dozen times. He was therefore curious to see his ultimate superior.

In the top man's office they were greeted cordially by the distinguished incumbent, who, having already occupied the post for nearly twenty-five years, looked as though he had been built into his surroundings. After shaking hands, and inviting his visitors to sit down, he said, "Well, gentlemen, I wanted to explain my thinking face-to-face. We have the two shootings in Liverpool Street, and it now seems clear that the first is connected to an ongoing case in Suffolk.

"But even if there weren't such a connection, this wouldn't be something I should want us to handle. It seems to me that the fact the murder took place on our patch is coincidental. I don't think there's any doubt the gunman was a professional. And the chance of him living – or even exclusively operating – in the square mile, is practically nil.

"We can't go roaming around the Met, so

we'd have to ask for their help anyway.

"Quite apart from that, I can't afford to have my officers working in the wilds of Suffolk. There's too much to do right here – and too few hands to do it all.

"I've spoken to the East Suffolk Chief Constable. He's of the same opinion: he can't have his men investigating in London. We've jointly requested that the Yard take it all on."

The Commissioner addressed the DI directly. "Playford, no doubt you'll be disappointed, but I hope you can accept the reasoning?"

"I can, sir. In fact I said much the same to my Sergeant earlier. I spoke to the Suffolk DI this morning, and he anticipated this decision as well."

"Good. DCI Bryce has been assigned to the case. He'll call into Bishopsgate on his way to Suffolk; you can expect him later this morning. You'll brief him, of course; and have whatever you've collected ready for him to pick up at the same time."

Handshakes concluded the meeting, and the two policemen were back at Bishopsgate within half an hour of leaving.

The Superintendent was pleased that significant resources wouldn't have to be diverted to this murder. The Inspector, however, felt a little differently. He couldn't fault the Commissioner's logic, and it was no exaggeration that he already had more than enough work on his own plate.

That said, murder cases within the square mile were not commonplace, and he wouldn't have minded the chance to work on this one.

Playford found an efficient-looking woman installed in his office when he returned. Peering through the half-moon spectacles nipping the bridge of her nose, she was working at his side table as he had instructed. A typewriter had been brought in, and she had the reporter's notebook open beside it. He was pleased to see everything else had been covered over and moved onto a cloth on the floor, the smell of disinfectant the only clue to the table's previous purpose.

The secretary paused in her work to lift her eyes above her glasses and smile at him.

"I'm Detective Inspector Playford," he said, and learned that she was Mrs Barbara Watkin.

"Has anyone offered you tea or coffee?" he enquired.

"Yes, thanks," came the bright response, "but I'm happy without for the moment.

"Your Sergeant asked me to interpret the shorthand in this notepad, and get it down into what he called 'understandable English'." She gave a little laugh. "Which is lucky, because that's the only kind of English I know!

"He suggested that I start at the most recent page and work backwards, but that's easier for him to say than it is for me to do, so I've gone to the beginning of the book.

"It's a newish pad, and there's not that many

pages filled in. It'll take me hardly any longer doing it that way round, and the result will be much more coherent for you." She flicked a finger at the sheets protruding from the top of the machine, causing them to fan out a little. "I've popped a couple of carbons in, so you'll have two copies plus the original."

Playford, impressed with Mrs Watkin's common-sense approach to her task, was rather less impressed with Phillips' instruction to her. "The Sergeant meant that anything earlier than a certain date doesn't interest us at the moment," he told the secretary. "But he obviously didn't explain that very well – or even give you the relevant date!

"The owner of this book was a reporter looking into a murder case. You can probably appreciate there may be important evidence in it."

Mrs Watkin gave a serious nod. "He – I assume it's a he – used Pitman's shorthand, but it's clear he didn't know it thoroughly, or else he's developed some unusual variations of his own.

"There are places I may have to guess what it says, but I'll always draw attention to those parts on the original by using the red half of the typewriter ribbon. When I do that, I'll annotate the carbons, so that everything corresponds with the top copy for you."

Playford was now more than satisfied that Marcus Cunningham's notepad was in safe hands. "A senior officer from Scotland Yard will be arriving to collect everything, including your transcript. Any chance it could all be done within the hour, so he doesn't have to hang about?"

"Oh, I'm sure I shall be finished before then; look, Inspector," Mrs Watkin leafed through the pad to show the remaining pages. "I'm a fair way through already, and there's very little in the later pages." She gave another smile and resumed her clacking at the machine, her fingers rapidly depressing the keys without moving her eyes from the reporter's notes.

Sitting at his desk, Playford called his Sergeant on the internal telephone. "It's all being passed to the Yard, as expected. DCI Bryce is coming to pick up everything we've got. What joy have you had with the photographs?"

Phillips explained these were still being processed, and would be delivered shortly. "When the photographs come, do you want me to start trawling round to see if any of the local villains recognises the gunman, sir?"

"No; not unless the Yard asks us to. Their resources are just a tad more extensive than ours – we'll leave it for them to organise. If the prints haven't arrived by the time Mr Bryce gets here, just get them to the Yard as soon as possible.

"The Desk Sergeant was on the telephone as I came in, so I didn't stop. Save me another job, Phillips, and just put your head out of your door to warn him that the Chief Inspector's arriving from the Yard at about eleven o'clock."

CHAPTER 3

At ten forty-five, two men walked into the Bishopsgate police station. The Desk Sergeant snapped to attention. "Ah, Chief Inspector Bryce, sir?"

"That's right, Sergeant; plus DS Haig. Mr Playford is expecting us."

"Yes, sir, he is. I'll show you up."

When the visiting Yard men had removed their overcoats and hats, Bryce, who had met the City DI before, introduced his Scottish Sergeant to him, and the three officers sat down together at the side table. The typewriter had been removed and the accumulated evidence again covered the table.

The Chief Inspector opened the conversation with a friendly question. "Well, Playford, how do you feel about us muscling in on your patch?"

"Taking it on the chin, sir – it's all I can do," laughed the local detective. "Completely inevitable, when you consider I'm hardly allowed to venture into the Met's patch, let alone all the way into Suffolk!"

The Yard detectives grinned.

"There's a coincidence in all this," said Bryce. "You didn't hear this conversation, Sergeant, but at the end of our Norfolk railway case I was talking to the two new partners in their office. They'd seen a report of the Ashton murder in the papers, and one said that I might soon be involved. I pooh-poohed the suggestion – yet a couple of days later here we are!

"Anyway, Inspector, tell us what's happened at this end."

Playford gave a summary of the situation, concluding by referencing the fingerprints and the photographs of the dead gunman, together with the witness statements, all of which – apart from the not-yet-delivered photographs – had now been collated into labelled manila folders.

"I haven't had time to look at all this, yet. My next job was to send someone with the prints to the Yard, to see if Records has a match. After that, I was going to get the best photos circulated to see if anyone – copper or criminal – recognised him. But I was summoned to HQ as soon as I arrived this morning, and the Commissioner said to hand everything over to you.

"To be honest, sir, I haven't even looked at the gun, which is in that big bundle. Fast asleep when I was called in last night, and by the time I'd looked at the bodies at the station, and then interviewed three witnesses, I was ready to drop.

Everything is here waiting for you, though," he said, as he indicated the folders on the table.

"Oh, one other thing: the reporter's notebook. All in shorthand, and might as well have been in Martian as far as I was concerned last night. But we've managed to get it written up this morning." He opened the folder holding Cunningham's notepad and three sheaves of foolscap sheets, each held together in the left-hand margin by treasury tags.

The DCI thought for a moment. Turning to Haig he said, "We're going to need someone over here to collect part of this evidence, Sergeant.

"Get hold of a DC. He can take the prints to Records first, and then arrange for distribution of the gunman's photograph when that arrives. Tell him he needs to get it into as many of the London papers as soon as he can; and prepare them all to do a re-run in a couple of days, in case we don't get much of a response from the first outing. The provincials will pick it all up from the London press, of course, although I'll discuss with Suffolk about getting it into the local papers quicker."

Bryce shot a question at Playford. "On the subject of identification, did Ipswich say anything about contacting Marcus Cunningham's family?"

"Yes, Inspector Catchpole said someone will be sent to break the news; he said he'd met Cunningham and knew where he lived."

"Good," responded Bryce. "We need to make sure his name isn't released until after we've managed to contact the next of kin. How he died will be shock enough, without reading it in a paper or hearing it on the wireless."

An afterthought occurred to Bryce. "Sergeant, tell whoever comes for the paperwork that they should also take the shotgun back and give it to the Armourer to lock away. Let's look at it ourselves, first."

Playford unrolled the truncated weapon from its sacking cover.

"Oh my word!" exclaimed Bryce as the gun was revealed. "I've heard of these, gentlemen, but never thought I'd ever get to see one. Have either of you?"

Both subordinates shook their heads.

"It's a Sauer Drilling; an M30 I think. Drilling means triplet, and as you can see, this has three barrels."

"German, then?" asked Haig as he leaned forwards to take a better look.

"Yes. They were apparently issued to Luftwaffe crews as survival weapons, particularly those operating over North Africa. Two 12-bore shotgun barrels; with a single large calibre rifle barrel underneath."

Playford looked baffled "Why would pilots, specifically, need a shotgun as well as a rifle, sir?"

"I believe the idea was that if they were shot down or ditched in difficult terrain, the shotgun would be used to pot birds and small game for food, with the rifle as protection against larger, more threatening animals."

Sergeant Haig, who had spent the war years in the police force, articulated what Playford (who had not seen military service either) was also thinking. "I've never even heard of a gun with three barrels, sir. I had no idea such things existed."

"I'm not surprised," said Bryce. "I believe these were originally privately ordered, possibly by Goering himself. They certainly weren't mass produced, and I hope we manage to find out how our assassin got hold of this one."

As he spoke, Bryce shook out his handkerchief and picked up the gun to examine its mechanism. "Beautiful piece of engineering. I can't see from the outside exactly how it works, but I believe it's possible to fire all three barrels via the two triggers without needing to break the gun between shots."

Playford, still staring in astonishment at the unusual weapon, wondered why the constable who brought it back to the station hadn't mentioned its extraordinary construction. Surely, when he pulled the gun out from under the assassin and broke it to remove the cartridges, he couldn't fail to notice the third barrel?

The DI remembered that PC Cowan had hesitated when asked if he knew how to break the gun, suggesting that the explanation for his lack of reaction was probably very straightforward – the constable may never have handled any sort of shotgun before, and therefore hadn't realised what an exceptional example the Drilling was. "There were no rifle rounds in the shooter's pockets – only the shotgun cartridges we have here with the gun," he told the Chief Inspector, and passed over a smaller bundle.

"Hmmm – two points to make about that," replied Bryce, opening the little parcel. "First, a sawn-off rifle makes little sense, because all accuracy would be sacrificed. But second, the calibre is a European one – 9.3 mm, I think. Probably hard to find a supply of bullets for it in this country."

The DCI, his fingers still protected by his handkerchief, held up one of the shotgun cartridges and examined it before casting his eye over the rest. "I'm not sure that these are commercially-produced cartridges anyway – our assassin may have prepared his own. I'd like to know what the load of shot is." He turned to his Sergeant. "Get the DC to ask the Armourer to open one up for me, please, and give his opinion."

Bryce wrapped up the gun and the cartridges again. "Do you anticipate the *post mortem* reports will come in later today, Inspector?"

"Yes, sir. Where do you want me to send them?"

"The Yard. I'll get someone to read them to me over the telephone. It'll be interesting to compare Mr Cunningham's with the Ashton PM report." Bryce nodded at his Sergeant, who was recording his Chief's instructions, to indicate that he had finished.

"May I use your telephone, sir?" Haig asked Playford.

"Help yourself, Sergeant."

As Haig moved across to Playford's desk to make his call to Scotland Yard, there was a tap on the door, and a uniformed officer came in bearing a large envelope. "Sent round by the photographer on the corner, sir," he said to the DI.

The City DI opened the envelope to take a careful look at the photographs of the gunman, while Bryce picked up a transcript of Marcus Cunningham's notebook.

Sergeant Phillips had taken pictures from four different angles, all of them acceptably clear. The two profiles showed the man had a large Roman nose and a full head of hair. His clean-shaven square jaw and thin lips, together with the fact that he was about thirty years old, were best observed in the two full-face photographs.

"I saw the shooter where he fell," said the local detective to Bryce, "and although the lighting on the concourse wasn't the best, I didn't recognise him last night. These are pretty good prints, though. Good enough for me to be certain that I've never seen him before."

"Same for me," said Bryce as he looked over the photographs. "But if he was the hired gun that we all believe him to be, I don't suppose he appeared in public very often to say 'cheese' to a camera! I doubt if he hung around with lesser criminals, either. I don't think we'll find many who do recognise him."

Sergeant Haig had finished issuing Bryce's orders. Hearing snippets of the conversation between the two senior detectives, and catching his Chief's last remark, he returned to his seat at the side table and offered up a thought to his superiors. "It all strikes me a wee bit Al Capone in style, if I can put it that way, sirs," he said, as he opened the folder nearest to him with Marcus Cunningham's ID. "Somehow it feels a not very British way of doing things – so a foreign national, maybe?"

"We'll certainly need to look into that possibility, if we can't turn up a home-grown villain," agreed Bryce, and went back to studying the transcript of Cunningham's notebook. Frowning at Playford, he asked, "Who deciphered and typed this for you?"

The City detective explained about Barbara Watkin's temporary recruitment. "Has she made a hash of it, sir?"

"No, not at all. Quite the reverse, in fact. She's drawn attention to something which obviously struck her as odd." He pushed the tagged bundle back towards the DI. "The top six pages deal with a series of interviews which Cunningham conducted in various locations on days *before* the murder in Ashton.

"Each of these earlier investigations has everything you'd expect – the date, time, and place; together with the detailed questions he asked people, and their responses more-or-less verbatim.

"He was very thorough in all those instances, even though the subject matter was mundane." Bryce reeled off a small selection of the petty incidents which the reporter had pursued: "A milk churn stolen from outside a dairy; a minor act of vandalism in a village hall; some accusations of nepotism at a parish council meeting."

He pulled back the sheaf and turned to the last three pages for Playford to see. "Here, however, when he's investigating the murder, there's no meaningful detail at all.

"He records the name of each person he speaks to and where he met them, but very little else. On the most recent pages, he doesn't even record what questions he asked; nor anything of what the interviewees said in reply. Very strange."

The DCI put the transcript back in the folder with the copies. "We'll take these, the ID and statements, and a couple of photographs of the gunman – maybe someone in Suffolk will recognise him." He loaded the folders into his briefcase and turned to Haig. "Everything explained to the help at the Yard, Sergeant?"

"Aye, sir, Barker is making a start on it. He'll be here within the hour to collect everything and do the necessary. Kittow is out at the moment, and won't be available until tomorrow, otherwise I'd have picked him."

"Good." Bryce stood up and buttoned his jacket over the waistcoat of his dark blue suit, then reached for his overcoat and hat. "Let's go across the road now, gentlemen."

The officers walked the short distance across Bishopsgate into the railway station, the local Inspector leading the way over the footbridge to the cafeteria. Again, there happened to be no train standing in Platform 9, and so from Lt Johnson's vantage point the three detectives were able to visualise what he had seen. Then, taking the same steps used he had done (but at a more measured pace) they reached the concourse below.

Nothing of the night's violence, remained visible, all the distressing evidence having been dealt with in the early hours of the morning. Playford nevertheless accurately identified the two crime scenes and, not for the first time in his career, silently praised the nameless and unseen workers who had carried out the necessary clean-up operations.

"Thank you Inspector," said Bryce, the picture of events completely clear in his mind. "We'll be off now, and leave you in peace. You'll still be involved, of course, as you have the two inquests at some point; and we'll be in touch to keep you informed of our progress."

Playford took the Chief Inspector's extended hand and smiled his thanks. "Anything you need that I can help with, sir, you know where to find me."

CHAPTER 4

The Yard men had been told that the Suffolk Detective Inspector would meet them at Woodbridge police station, it being the nearest to Ashton village where the murder had been committed.

Bryce, who knew the roads through the East End of London well, drove the Wolseley via Bethnal Green and Stratford to reach the A12. Passing through Chelmsford and Colchester, they paused for a quick lunch in a roadside pub outside the latter town. Haig took the wheel for the rest of the journey through Ipswich, and onwards up the A12 to the little town of Woodbridge and its police station.

The detectives were greeted by a Desk Sergeant who looked as though his retirement was well overdue. However, he was alert enough, coming to attention and giving a polite welcome to the officers in a delightful Suffolk accent.

"The DI is expecting you, gentlemen. We've found him a room, if you'd care to come with me."

He tapped on a door, and held it open for the

Yard officers.

"Welcome back to Suffolk, sir! It's pleasure to see you again," came the hearty greeting from a young officer in plain clothes as he moved from behind his table with outstretched hand.

"Good to see you too, Inspector," said Bryce. "This is Alex Haig – you know him by name, of course, as he was involved with the London end of your Felixstowe case."

"Yes indeed," said Catchpole, shaking hands with the Sergeant. "I'll be seeing you both at the trial in a few weeks, no doubt. I expect you know that it was postponed from one Assizes because of legal arguments, so matters have dragged on a bit, but it should go ahead at the next."

"You must bring us up to date later," said the DCI, "over dinner tonight, perhaps, if you're available?"

"Yes, thank you, sir," replied the DI, pulling forwards chairs for his visitors.

"Brief us on your village murder then, Catchpole," said Bryce as he sat back and crossed his legs.

The local detective laid his hand on a pile of papers. "Well, this little heap contains the *post mortem* report, and some disappointing tell-us-nothing statements.

"The deceased is George Wilcox, a retired solicitor. Sixty-six years old and a widower. He was shot on Wednesday afternoon while working in his garden, which backs onto woods. Wilcox was one of only two people who had the consent of the owner to shoot over the land – that's extensive woodland plus quite a few fields, apparently. I'll come back to the other chap in a moment.

"When the body was found, the first assumption was that he was killed by a stray shot, either by the other shooting rights-holder or by a poacher. Accident was quickly ruled out, because the shot was fired at very close range.

"Also, the *post mortem* shows the cartridge used was loaded with LG shot, and our police surgeon reckons the entire load hit Wilcox's chest."

"Sorry, sir," interrupted Haig, looking at his Yard superior. "Can you just explain this thing about the shot, and how it's significant?"

"Yes, of course. The lead pellets in a shotgun cartridge are sized using the old vocabulary for musket ammunition – grapeshot. So LG is 'large grapeshot'.

"Nowadays, the size of lead pellet for LG is such that there are roughly six pellets per ounce. Americans call it 000Buck, which perhaps gives a clue about usage.

"There are various pellet weights. SG – 'small grapeshot' – is eight per ounce, and SSG is even smaller at fifteen or so per ounce. With only six to the ounce you can appreciate that LG, comparatively speaking, is a very hefty pellet."

Haig nodded his understanding. "What did the Drilling we saw in London hold?" he asked.

"It was chambered for a short, two and a half inch, cartridge. That means if LG shot was used, that size of cartridge might hold only six or so pellets.

"It's perhaps easier to understand when you know that far lighter pellets – around two hundred per ounce – are the sort typically used for bird shooting nowadays, and of course many more of those fit into a cartridge."

Bryce turned back to the local DI. "Go on, Catchpole."

"The shot was heard by several people, but because it's countryside and shooting is common enough, nobody took any notice. It was about three hours later when a couple of lads, walking along the path beside the wood, saw Wilcox lying on the ground just inside his garden. They went to take a closer look. There's only a post and wire fence with a simple gate – which was standing open.

"The boys realised he was dead. They ran around the side of the house to the front, and raised the alarm.

"The second holder of shooting rights, Desmond Allen, is a retired diplomat, sixty-nine years old. Another widower, and he also lives in the village.

"The two were apparently quite close friends – they had a regular drink in the local pub once a week, that sort of thing. The locals tell me they'd had an agreement for years; Allen could shoot on Mondays, Wednesdays, and Fridays, and Wilcox on Tuesdays, Thursdays, and Saturdays. In practice, though, each only went shooting perhaps once a fortnight. Apparently they didn't go shooting together.

"The problem we have is that Allen has disappeared. He isn't at home – or at least he isn't answering his door bell or his telephone. He has a cleaner every Friday, but she only works when he's in the house, and doesn't have a key. We've spoken to her, and she has no knowledge of his whereabouts.

"I went to request a warrant this morning, citing the possibility that he might have shot his friend, and the fact that he's disappeared. I had to admit, of course, that Wilcox's injuries didn't look as though they were from a shotgun loaded for a simple bit of rough shooting – and that's all Allen ever does, as far as is known. I also said that we were trying to contact his son who lives in London."

"I'm guessing you weren't successful with your application," said Bryce.

"No. The JP was sympathetic, but refused to grant a warrant. He pointed out, reasonably enough, that Allen may just be away for a few days, and that there was no requirement for him to have told anyone. He did say that if we can't find him, or a relative, within twenty-four hours I can go back and ask again.

"We've had to content ourselves for the

moment by pushing a note through Allen's letterbox, asking him to urgently telephone as soon as he comes home – day or night.

"However, we succeeded in locating the son just before you arrived. Bernard Allen is a civil servant in Whitehall, but unfortunately is away on official business in Edinburgh at the moment. I've been able to speak to him, though. He's coming to Ashton, but doesn't expect to arrive until after midnight; says we can see him first thing tomorrow morning."

"Did the son say he knew where his father was?" asked Haig.

"No, he had no idea his father wasn't at home, but that wasn't unusual because they weren't in constant contact. He said his father had taken short holidays before, and the first the son knew about it was when he got a postcard from Rhyl, or wherever.

"Why do I get the impression you don't really think Allen senior is a likely suspect for Wilcox's murder?" asked Bryce.

Catchpole shook his head, filled his cheeks, and then exhaled. "For no better reason than it just doesn't feel right to me, especially not now that I've heard about the second shooting in London.

"Up until Playford rang this morning, I couldn't rule out that Allen might have shot his friend and then scarpered – which was why I wanted a warrant, of course. But for an elderly man to carry out two murders in pretty quick succession – the second of which sounds like a well-organised ambush – no, I can't buy that."

The young Inspector looked piercingly at Bryce. "Do you have photographs of the London gunman yet, sir? Or, if not, a good description of him?" he asked. "We could rule Allen in or out pretty easily that way."

The Chief Inspector smiled. On hearing Allen senior was approaching seventy he had immediately eliminated the Ashton man as the London shooter. He was pleased that Catchpole's intuition was good, and pulled out the photographs for the local Inspector. "As you see, our gunman is in his thirties – probably closer to Allen's son in age, rather than Allen himself."

"Not someone I recognise, sir," said Catchpole. "But we'll definitely circulate his picture up here."

"We still need to locate Allen, though, don't we, sirs?" asked Haig, "because it's possible that he's the one who paid the assassin to do the dirty work while he kept his own hands clean."

Bryce nodded. "Agreed. And having heard that Allen had the shooting rights on Wednesdays – the day that Wilcox was shot – we have another possibility: that Allen came across the gunman in the woods, and never came out again. What have you done about searching the woods and fields, Catchpole?"

"Nothing as yet, sir. We're woefully short of men, and that's on top of suffering from the same increases in crime seen elsewhere since the war. As soon as the son told me his father would take off on occasion without mentioning the fact, I felt I had no choice but to hang fire for the moment."

Bryce nodded. "I think you've made a reasonable decision, given the constraints on resources. Here's hoping Allen's son confirms his father's suitcase and sponge bag have gone." He thought a little. "Be as well if you ask the younger Allen to let you know if one of his father's guns is missing though, if a suitcase isn't. That information would also tell us a great deal.

"In the meantime, Catchpole, tell us about Wilcox."

"He used to be partner in a firm of solicitors in Ipswich. Specialised in wills and probate. Quite an authority in his field, and apparently consulted by other firms on occasion. He didn't touch criminal work at all, so I never ran into him professionally.

"He only retired a few months ago. He'd lived in Ashton for twenty-odd years. No one had any fulsome praise for him, but equally, there was absolutely no suggestion of naked enmity directed at him from any quarter.

Bryce nodded. "Do you know what Wilcox did in his spare time when he wasn't shooting or in the pub?"

"Well, sir, there's only limited opportunity for a social circle in a small village, of course. I'm told he and his wife used to entertain a bit now and then, played bridge, and did all the usual things. He also sat on the Parochial Church Council; but since his wife died about eighteen months ago, he seems to have withdrawn more and more. He resigned from the PCC, and no longer accepted bridge invitations. Still did some rough shooting on his own, but stopped drinking with Allen in the local and, of late, even turned down invitations to formal shoots.

"As nobody in the village saw anyone in the road at the front of the house – and no strange car either – we've assumed that the killer came through the wood, and left the same way."

"How extensive is the wood, sir?" asked Haig.

"I'm told it's over forty acres in total. Mostly deciduous with a few pines, and the odd clearing. Some dense undergrowth in places. There's a road on the far side away from any houses; very little used, though, and there are places where anyone could drive a short distance into the wood, then park almost out of sight. The chances of someone passing that way and spotting anything would be low – especially if the car was a dark colour, or had a few branches pulled over it for camouflage."

"Is there a guard on Wilcox's house?" asked Bryce.

Catchpole shook his head. "We had a good look and there was nothing of any use for us, but no doubt you'll want to see for yourselves as well."

Sergeant Haig put another question. "We

understand you came across Cunningham during your investigations, sir?"

"That's right; he said he had a cottage in the village and he took a proprietorial interest in the case. He approached me asking for a statement as soon as I arrived on the scene, but I wasn't ready to make one at that stage.

"He found me again the next morning, and I gave him the basics then. I knew he was still poking around – my Sergeant was interviewing a villager earlier, and he told me Cunningham turned up also wanting to ask her questions. I'd seen him several times walking around Ashton, and he gave me his address readily enough when I asked. And of course he wasn't breaking any law by interviewing people."

Catchpole spread his hands. "That pretty much sums it up from this end. And as much as it's a kick in the teeth for me if a reporter managed to trump my own efforts investigating Wilcox's murder, as soon as I heard this morning that Cunningham had been shot, my first thought was that he must have got hold of something important."

The young Inspector turned down the corners of his mouth and pulled a glum face before admitting, "Either I haven't come across that important something yet – or I've already overlooked it and you'll have to point it out to me, sir!"

This was the open and willing to learn

attitude which had impressed Bryce earlier in the year, when he had been honeymooning in Felixstowe and first met the young Ipswich DI. He acknowledged the younger man's rueful comment with a nod, before outlining his investigation plans.

"Later today I'd like to go through all the statements you've acquired, Catchpole. I'll be doing the same with the paperwork from the Liverpool Street shootings. We have transcripts of Cunningham's shorthand from the notepad he was carrying, as well as statements from two witnesses and the army chap who took out the gunman.

"We've had a quick look at all the London paperwork in the car, but I can tell you that at first glance Cunningham's shorthand notes seem to be useless." He opened his briefcase and handed a carbon copy of the transcript to Catchpole. "Just names and addresses of people recorded as 'residents'; and an appointment next week at Wilcox's old firm in Ipswich.

"You'll need to go through all of that yourself; but my first impression is that there's nothing finger-pointing – much less incriminating – in what we've got. Not even a mention of why Cunningham travelled to London at that time of night."

"Must have been by arrangement, sir, for the gunman to be there to meet his train," remarked Haig.

"Yes indeed. And his return ticket implies that he didn't expect to stay long. Let's hope that we'll find some clue in his house or office. I take it he was on *The Anglian Examiner*?"

"Yes, sir."

"Has anyone been to speak to staff?"

Catchpole shook his head. "Not yet. Playford and I agreed that the reporter's name wouldn't be released until after we'd found his next of kin. I'm to tell him when we've done that. I arranged for a constable to go to Cunningham's home as soon as I heard the news this morning. He was to inform any family he could find and let me know when he'd done so. I told him if no one was in he should wait until someone showed up – and say nothing to anyone else about why he was there. I've not heard anything from him yet."

"Even if there's someone at home, I've told him to stay there on guard anyway. If there's any evidence in the cottage, I want us to find it before whoever wanted him dead tries to get hold of it. The village telephone box is on the corner of the road, so easy enough for my officer to call me and still keep an eye on the cottage.

"The next step was going to be informing the newspaper of their reporter's death, and asking questions."

Bryce was again pleased with the local Inspector's reasoning. Satisfied that he and Haig had been fully briefed, he was ready to move things forward. "The fact that it's Sunday means there will only be a skeleton staff at the *Examiner's* offices, and that's less helpful to us. But I'm sure there'll be someone who can at least supply contact details of more knowledgeable people, if need be.

"Here's what I want to happen today. Your first job, Inspector, is to get someone around to the newspaper and talk to whoever is there, because it's after two o'clock already and we can't wait indefinitely until his family have been notified.

"Whoever goes to the paper should check if Cunningham spoke to a colleague about his Liverpool Street assignment – particularly whether they know if he received a telephone call at the office about it.

"Also, give a photograph of the gunman to the paper and ask them to print it as soon as possible with a suitable 'have you seen this man?' caption.

"The three of us will take a look at Cunningham's cottage, and the murder scene."

Bryce pulled Cunningham's keys out of his pocket as he outlined the final task. "There's an ignition key here," he said as he eased it off the ring and handed it to Catchpole. "It's a fair bet he drove to the station to take the train. Should be straightforward for your men to get a description of the car from someone at the office; after which they should go to the station car park and one of them can retrieve it. I suppose Cunningham might have started out from Woodbridge station, but obviously they should check Ipswich first as they're already there."

Bryce turned to Haig. "Sergeant, call DC Barker at the Yard and see if he has any news for us yet.

"While you two are getting on with that, I may as well make a start looking at your paperwork, Inspector."

It took barely five minutes for Catchpole to delegate his allotted tasks. "I've given the press office job to DS Jephson and DC Payne. You met Jephson in Felixstowe, sir," he said. "He's a good man."

Haig, who had gone to use the telephone at the front desk, was also soon finished. "Barker was there, sir. He collected the gun and cartridges from Bishopsgate, and delivered the lot to the Armourer as instructed. Apparently, Inspector Bailey's reaction when he saw the gun was much the same as yours. Barker said Mr Bailey used very rude words to describe someone who would cut down any gun, but especially anyone who would ruin such a classic. He'll open a couple of the cartridges, and test fire a few as well. Your secretary will get the report.

"Multiple copies of the gunman's photograph are being processed, and they'll go out to all divisions today, for detectives and beat bobbies. Each division will show the picture to their known ne'er-do-wells – emphasising that the gunman's dead. Hopefully that fact will loosen a tongue or two which might otherwise be too frightened to wag.

"Oh, and Records don't have his prints."

"A pity, but as we expected," said Bryce as he stood up. "I'd like to get over to Ashton now, whilst there's still good daylight left. Travel with us, Catchpole, and you can give directions to Cunningham's house.

It took only ten minutes to reach Ashton. They passed a sadly dilapidated and apparently unoccupied row of stone cottages as the car entered the village. "Cunningham's isn't one of these," commented Catchpole. "His is of a completely different construction, although it looks to be in equally poor condition. That's George Wilcox's house, by the way," he continued, pointing out an altogether superior detached house a little further on.

"The village was never large, I should think, but since the war the numbers – especially of young people – have dropped in places like this. Apart from any losses in the war, there isn't so much labour needed on the land, or even in service, I suppose; people move away to the towns to find work or when they marry; and then there's the £10 scheme to encourage emigration to Australia."

"Yes; interesting scheme. Very apposite slogan they came up with: 'Populate or Perish'. New Zealand has followed suit now, I see."

The DI directed Haig to turn into a side road

and the local Inspector identified the journalist's cottage – standing in its own plot, but close beside a terrace of four others. The terraced cottages were similar to the ones noted a few minutes earlier, in grey stone with slate roofs, but these appeared to be occupied. Cunningham's had rendered walls, washed in a pale and grimy shade of 'Suffolk pink', and roofed with thatch. A uniformed constable stood by the door, his bicycle leaning against the gate.

Haig parked the Wolseley in front of the property and pointed at the local authority sign fixed to the front garden wall, which proclaimed that the road name was Old Loke. He looked over his shoulder at his two superiors.

"If this is Cunningham's house, it's not the address on his ID card."

CHAPTER 5

Bryce was also puzzled. "You're right, Sergeant. Fonnerau Road was the address in his ID." He turned to the local detective. "Playford told us you already knew the address, Catchpole."

Catchpole cast his mind back to the conversation with his Bishopsgate counterpart in order to unscramble the misunderstanding, and soon realised how it had occurred.

"It's true that when Playford told me Marcus Cunningham's name I said immediately that I already knew him, and where he lived." He shook his head regretfully. "Thinking about it, Playford didn't mention an address after that – there was no reason to. And this is definitely the address Cunningham gave me."

"Do you know where Fonnerau Road is?" asked Bryce.

"It's in Ipswich, sir, a good twelve miles away. Expensive houses beside Christchurch Park. A very far cry from this place. I can only think he must have moved, sir, and not changed his ID."

"Perhaps. Or else he lied to you. Or he has

two homes. But most likely the Ipswich one is his parents' house," said Bryce, pulling out the key ring with the two remaining keys. "We'll soon find out. Let's see if one of these fits."

The three men climbed out of the car and were greeted by the police guard, who reported that he had seen no occupants. Catchpole told the Constable he could stand down, and return to his normal duties in the neighbouring village where he was stationed.

The officers took a good look at the exterior of the little house. It was a little larger than its terraced neighbours, but looked to be significantly more dilapidated. The thatched roof was in a very poor condition. The exterior paintwork on walls and woodwork was equally neglected, the front window frames so rotten in places that Bryce doubted if they could be saved.

Trying the first of the two remaining keys on the ring, the Chief Inspector found it unlocked the front door.

Inside the door was a tiny hallway, barely large enough for one man to occupy at a time. To right and left were doorways, but neither had a door. Bryce ducked to avoid hitting his head on the low door beam as he stepped down inside, and was astonished to find he was standing on a dirt floor. Compacted after countless years of being walked over, the surface was firm and smooth and almost polished-looking under foot.

Haig, following, remarked in surprise that

the cottage seemed smaller on the inside than its external dimensions suggested.

"It's the clay lump, Sergeant; or 'clump', as we call it," explained Catchpole. "It's an ancient construction material in East Anglia; a mixture of clay and straw, with a bit of dung thrown in. It was shaped into bricks that were dried but unbaked. Quite a bit bigger than a standard, kiln-fired brick. Most houses using this construction aren't large to begin with, but the walls are so thick that the interiors always feel much smaller than you expect from the outside."

The left-hand doorway led to a kitchen, and the detectives entered this room first. A battered chest of cupboards stood against the far wall. Sitting on top was a breadboard holding part of a brown loaf, with a covered butter dish beside it. Bending to open the six doors, Bryce found two tins of corned beef in one, a frying pan holding several apples in another, and some cutlery and a packet of dried egg in a third. The remaining cupboards were empty.

Shelves above the chest held a few plates and a tea caddy, with cups hanging from hooks beneath the lower shelf. Once, there had been an open fireplace in the room, on which presumably any cooking had been done. At some later date – although still many years ago, Bryce judged – a pot-bellied coal stove had been fitted, its single hotplate apparently the only means of heating food, or water for cooking and washing. The flue pipe of the stove had been crudely fed into the original chimney. Two metal rings encircling the flue pipe were fixed to the chimney breast behind, a bone-dry dish cloth and tea towel hanging from one. As a simple means of drying and airing washing it had something to recommend it, Bryce thought, but only if it had been possible to shut the door and prevent the water vapour from penetrating the rest of the house.

"No gas in the village," remarked Catchpole, seeing the DCI eyeing the arrangements, "and electricity hasn't reached every house yet."

There was a door at the far side of the kitchen, and Catchpole, standing closest, opened it but didn't enter the tiny room beyond. The Yard detectives, peering past him, could now see the only concession to modernity in the property – an extension, which looked to be a recent addition, housing a lavatory.

Haig, much surprised by the condition of the rest of the cottage, half expected to see squares of the reporter's own newspaper impaled on a nail, but saw instead a roll of Izal hanging from a wooden holder. Above this was a small window for ventilation, overlooking the rear.

Standing by the wooden draining board of the chipped ceramic sink, Bryce wasn't surprised to see it had only one tap. Pulling aside the shabby length of curtain beneath, he confirmed his suspicion that there would be a bucket to catch waste water from the sink, rather than any plumbed pipework.

"A tank on the back wall must be feeding this tap with cold water, instead of the rising mains," he remarked. "And there must be a similar arrangement for the toilet cistern, with a pump or well outside to collect the water to supply both tanks." He shook his head. "What a chore!"

Catchpole agreed. "One of the downsides of living in the more rural parts of the country. There'll be a septic tank or, more likely, a soakaway at the bottom of the garden for the WC."

The officers moved via the 'hall' to look in the living room. Haig, finding there was hardly space for him to join his colleagues, instead investigated what looked like a cupboard facing the front door. Finding that it actually gave access to the stairs, he went through. Within a minute he returned, and standing in the doorway reported his findings.

"Watch yourselves if you go up there, sirs," he cautioned. It's a very narrow and steep stairway – and you have to really squeeze through the space just below where the two chimneys meet at the top. Nothing in one bedroom, and nothing of any interest in the other," he added. "Either Mr Cunningham led a very simple life, or he didn't really live here at all."

Bryce and Catchpole continued to look around the tiny living room. A desk and chair took up much of the available space, with an ancient leather armchair and a small closed gate-leg table also squeezed in.

An open fireplace beside the armchair, ash in its little grate, caused the DCI to pause and wonder if the room became any more homely with a good blaze on its hearth. The presence of a long-handled brass fork, hanging from a nail, suggested toasted bread or crumpets might be made and enjoyed. He doubted if that comfort would be enough to lift most people's spirits when the many privations of the little dwelling were weighed in the balance.

The house and its contents were certainly rudimentary – apart, that was, from the telephone. In these primitive conditions the black instrument sat most incongruously on top of the desk which Catchpole was now searching. Bryce had noticed the telegraph pole, its solitary wire connecting to the cottage, as soon as the Wolseley had turned into The Old Loke. Given the lengthy waiting list for a telephone, he assumed that either the *Anglian Examiner*, or Cunningham himself, must have had some 'pull' – although with the public kiosk already sited nearby the actual cost of connection had probably not been very high.

The desk, like the chest of cupboards in the kitchen, was practically empty. The only item of possible relevance to the investigation was lying on the top. Catchpole passed the scribbled note to the Chief Inspector. It read:

'10:40 by p6. 10 min. max. Ips 9:12 up 11 back worth it'.

"Looks like this is what took him to London, sir," said Catchpole, handing over the note.

Bryce nodded sombrely as he read it.

"There's hardly room for us all in here," he continued, passing the reporter's note to Haig. "I'll take a quick look upstairs and outside whilst you start knocking on neighbouring doors and talk to whoever you can find, Sergeant. Listen to any gossip, of course, and I'll come out and join you shortly. And you can tell whoever you speak to that Cunningham is dead."

Haig and Catchpole both looked surprised at the change of direction regarding the news about Cunningham. Bryce explained why he was releasing the information of the reporter's murder before his next of kin had been informed. "Not a decision that I've taken lightly; but it's Sunday afternoon and a calculated risk for me that his family can be contacted before anything reaches them through other channels."

He issued orders to the local DI. "Take our car, Catchpole, and sort out a visit to Fonnereau Road. The house number was sixty-something – which narrows it down well enough for you. I'm chancing that there'll be someone home at that address – and that you'll be able to break the news to them before it starts to radiate out of the village from whoever we speak to here.

"Go via Woodbridge, and send someone to pick us up. We'll be taking a look at the woods to the rear of Wilcox's property by then, so whoever you send to collect us will find us there."

Taking the Wolseley's keys from Haig, Catchpole made his way back to the car as Haig opened the gate of the house next door.

Alone in Cunningham's cottage, Bryce climbed the steep and narrow stairway to the upper floor, and found it as Haig had reported. He thought that a person of even moderate girth would have difficulty squeezing between the two chimney breasts. Humans were quite a bit smaller when this cottage was built, perhaps two hundred years ago, he thought. He found an unmade bed and a small bedside cabinet holding a torch and spare batteries in one of what were little more than attic rooms. An open suitcase under the bed contained dirty laundry, reinforcing the impression that this was not the reporter's permanent home.

In each bedroom room the ceiling was darkly stained in places where the leaking roof had allowed rain to enter, and in the unused bedroom some areas of plaster had already fallen away to reveal semi-rotten wooden laths.

He stood facing a tiny window in quiet contemplation for a while. The fact that Cunningham, who had a home elsewhere, should rent such a poor property – it was barely habitable – struck him as most odd. He could think of no good reason why the reporter would have done so, and he thought that Cunningham's tenure of the cottage must surely be significant.

With nothing further to see, he returned to the ground floor and ducked his head again as he left the cottage. After locking the front door, he walked around to the rear.

The garden was extensive, but overgrown, apart from where someone had quite recently dug what he assumed was the soakaway for the toilet. He saw a water pump, a coal bunker, and an old privy shack, its wooden box toilet now made redundant by the indoor WC. Beyond that there was nothing but weeds to be seen.

Returning to the front, he saw Haig talking to three women. He walked to the top of the Old Loke to join his Sergeant, quickly assessing the make-up of the group as he approached. From their dress and appearance he judged that one was from the more affluent class.

"This is Chief Inspector Bryce, from Scotland Yard," Haig told them.

The villagers nodded a welcome, and chorused a polite 'good afternoon' to him.

"I've been trying to allay the residents' fears about Mr Wilcox's murder sir," said Haig, "and I've explained about Mr Cunningham and why the gunman won't be coming back here – or anywhere else."

"Good," approved Bryce, "I hope you'll pass that information on around the village, ladies. You can tell anyone you care to that as yet we don't know why Mr Wilcox and Mr Cunningham suffered the fate they did – but we will find out.

"I presume none of you saw anyone behaving suspiciously in the village – or a strange car – either on the day Mr Wilcox was killed, or some time before?"

Three heads moved from side to side.

"Mr Cunningham spoke to me and to other people in Ashton since George's murder," said the most affluent-looking lady, who introduced herself as Christina Fielding.

Both detectives immediately recognised her name as one of those recorded by Marcus Cunningham, but neither mentioned the fact. Haig enquired after the other two ladies' names and knew that they hadn't appeared in the reporter's notebook.

"Did Mr Cunningham play any sort of active role in the village since he moved here?" asked Haig.

"Not really," Mrs Fielding again answered for the group. "You evidently know he took one of these cottages. He rented from Mr Eddington, who owns quite a bit of land hereabouts, but lives the other side of the county. I should think Vincent Eddington fairly jumped for joy when Mr Cunningham took the lease."

Nods from the two other women supported this opinion.

"But Mr Cunningham only arrived a few months ago, and he didn't live here you know – just came for an occasional night or weekend, I gather." More nods from her companions indicated this was also their understanding. "I'd only seen him two or three times myself, before all this."

"I seed him, on and off," said the oldest of the three women. "I said to my Bert, he durst not live in that cottage when the winter damp sets in. And my Bert, he say to me 'That Mr Eddington dun't put a penny piece into the upkeep o' that property; there's not another cottage hereabouts dun't have pamment floors a hundred year ago. I believes Mr Cunningham is more like campin' in there,' is what my Bert said."

Bryce smiled and politely agreed with 'my Bert's opinion'. Nothing more was forthcoming, so he thanked the three women. "We may need to talk to you all again in future, but in the meantime, please contact us if you think of anything which might help, and tell anyone else you speak to that they should do the same."

The little group dispersed.

Bryce reviewed with Haig what they had discovered so far. "Well, we've confirmed that Cunningham did receive a call, so that's as we thought, and it's clear that he was set up for his own execution. But that's as much as we've got from his cottage – not exactly a haul, Sergeant, and I have to say I'm disappointed. I hope you had a bit more joy with his neighbours than we've just had with those three ladies."

The Sergeant shook his head. "No response at two of the cottages, and the occupants of the other two could tell me nothing."

A pair of men now appeared in the distance, and the detectives walked back down The Old Loke to intercept them. They met as the older man opened the gate to the slightly larger and significantly better-maintained cottage next door to Cunningham's.

"Ah, sirs, does you want to talk to me?" asked the ancient. "You'm the police, I reckon. Summat's up, I know, on account of Fred Judd loiterin' about next door all day and not sayin' why. I'm Spraggons. Does you want to ask me summat?"

Bryce explained to the two men that the reporter had been killed. The young man gasped in horrified astonishment at the news, but the old boy didn't turn a hair. Advanced age had become a form of inoculation against the shock of death for him. He had buried two wives and four of his nine children; the passing of a little-known neighbour was something he could take in his stride very easily.

"A regular rum 'un, 'e was. 'E just come when he wanted, in his little motor. Always 'ad a chat wi' me, though, very polite. I seed him in the Oak a few times, he used to drop in even afore he took next door. Never touched his garden, though, and I told him, clear enough, what needed doing to make ready for winter and spring planting. He warn't interested, though."

"What sort of car did he drive?" asked Haig. He knew that Catchpole's man, Jephson, was tasked with discovering the reporter's vehicle, but it occurred to him that since Cunningham had two addresses, he might also have two cars.

"Ah, no use you lookin' at me for that sort o' clever knowledge," laughed the old boy. "Lucky for you my grandson from Ipswich is here – Samuel Yarries he be. He'll tell you good enough."

"That's right, sir," interposed the young man eagerly. A good foot taller than the old man, their kinship was nevertheless obvious. He spoke with the engaging zeal of an enthusiast as he quickly gave details of Cunningham's vehicle. "It were a green Morris Eight, Series E, two door saloon from mebbee 1938.

"Not the best car in the world today, o' course, but being as I don't have a motor myself, and how I do dearly wish for one, I'd have taken it off his hands in a heartbeat – if he'd give it me!"

As with the women, neither man could provide any information to advance the investigation. The Chief Inspector thanked them and issued the usual instruction about contacting the police. The detectives walked away, leaving Spraggons and his grandson still chatting outside.

Bryce surveyed the sky; twilight was gathering. "Let's find Wilcox's place now, Haig, and take a look at the ground where he was killed."

Walking back to the village main road, they cut across the green and walked until they found the house which Catchpole had pointed out to them. Standing with fields to one side, and the wood immediately behind it, was a fair-sized property. As its name, *The Pightle,* suggested, it was positioned on an oddly shaped plot.

"A wonderful piece of history and an old English word right here in the name of this house," said Bryce appreciatively. "It will have been some sort of agricultural land once, centuries ago. But when it became uneconomic to husband smaller, irregular spurs to the main fields, other uses were found for these little 'pigtails' or 'pightles' of land."

Haig was immediately taken by the explanation of the unfamiliar word. "It's my job to put the ribbons on the ends of wee Rosie's pigtails when I'm at home," he said. "I'll be calling them pightles from now on, and keeping the old English alive."

"Only the ribbons, Sergeant? Fiona doesn't allow you to do the plaiting at all?" queried Bryce in mock disbelief. He was fond of the Sergeant's bright little four-year-old, and had hoped more than once that he and Veronica might one day have such an animated young spark themselves.

"She says I'm too slow – and Rosie says I'm too clumsy!"

The Chief Inspector laughed as he indicated that they should walk down one side of the house. The detectives were soon standing in the garden behind, where four stakes in the ground marked out the crime scene.

"Right up against the fence here, sir, with only a strand of wire between him and the footpath," said the Sergeant. "And only a few steps from the wood beyond the path."

The combination of proximity to the wood, and the lack of more substantial fencing or hedging, meant that the view of the wood from the house was uninterrupted. This would doubtless be a magnificent prospect throughout the year as the seasons changed. But the corollary was that this situation had also made the assassin's work much easier.

Bryce walked through the open gate and stood on the path which ran between garden and wood. He looked back at the garden, and called his observations to Haig.

"I must be roughly on the spot from which the gunman fired. The trees in the next garden completely block the windows in that house. No other properties are visible beyond the immediate neighbour. The only way anyone could see the shooter is if they happened to be walking along this footpath, which judging by the undergrowth doesn't look to be much used."

"Assuming the gunman wasn't lucky enough to find Wilcox already in his garden, all he had to do was wait just inside the trees. Even somebody coming along the path wouldn't see him – but he'd still be able to see into the garden.

"An ideal spot for committing murder and getting away with it," he remarked, as he came back through the gate.

There was nothing more to be seen, and twilight was giving way to darkness. A car could be heard slowing in the road and Bryce said, "Let's see if that's our lift."

The Yard detectives were soon seated in the back of the police car. On the way back to Woodbridge, Bryce invited Haig to give his views on the case so far.

"The first question in my mind is whether the assassin was acting for himself, or on behalf of a third party, sir. And I'm wondering if that may depend on the background of the gunman – when we find out who he is. If it turns out he has any sort of previous form, then I'm sure that he was hired, and for both jobs.

"My next question would be whether he was hired to shoot anyone else after Wilcox and Cunningham. I know we're reassuring everyone that the gunman is in the morgue and can't go after anyone else – which is true, of course. But that doesn't stop his paymaster fixing up a substitute, does it?"

"No, you're absolutely right," said Bryce grimly. "Cunningham was going to speak to someone at Wilcox's firm this coming week. It's the only contact outside of the village that he recorded and we'll follow it up ourselves tomorrow, and see where it takes us."

Arriving at Woodbridge police station, the detectives made their way to Catchpole's incident room and were surprised to see that the local Inspector had arrived before them. Catchpole explained.

"I called in to swap cars and hand over your car keys, and to see if Sergeant Jephson had left any messages. I'd literally just stepped in the door as the Desk Sergeant's telephone rang.

"Jephson was checking whether Payne should take Cunningham's car to Ipswich police station or bring it here to Woodbridge. When he told me that they'd thoroughly inspected it, I said he should drive it to Fonnereau Road and break the news to any family there at the same time.

"He's done that, sir. I've just heard back from him again, and got his preliminary report."

"Good," said Bryce. "Let's hear what your men had to say."

Catchpole read from his notes. "The weekend duty reporter at the newspaper knew nothing of Cunningham's trip to London. However, he'd taken a personal call for Cunningham at the office at about six o'clock yesterday evening. He knew Cunningham was intending to stay in Ashton that night, and so gave the caller that telephone number.

"He was sure the call was made from a public call box, but unfortunately he was vague about what the caller sounded like. He said the voice sounded muffled, and it was a terrible line anyway. He gave a good description of Cunningham's car, though.

"Jephson and Payne had no trouble finding the vehicle at Ipswich station and thoroughly searched it. The vehicle was, quote, *'... in good order; contained only one old driving glove, and absolutely nothing of interest to our investigation...'."*

The Yard detectives learned that Jephson and Payne had each taken a car and driven to the top of Fonnereau Road. A resident who recognised the reporter's car told them that Cunningham lived with his mother at number 68.

Jephson, with Payne in attendance, performed the unpleasant duty of informing Mrs Cunningham of her son's death, arranging for a neighbour to sit with her when they left '...*as the time was not right for questioning the bereaved and thoroughly distressed lady*.'

Jephson had returned to Ipswich police station with Payne, and concluded his report with confirmation that he had advised the City Force that Cunningham's next of kin had now been informed.

"That's several jobs well done by your men," said Bryce, thoroughly satisfied. "After dinner this evening, I'll shut myself away in my room and read all the paperwork; then I'll plan what we're all doing tomorrow.

"On the subject of dinner, Catchpole, where are you billeting us tonight?" he enquired.

"You have rooms at The Bull, on Market Hill, sir. You saw the Royal Oak in Ashton as we passed, but that's a pub, not an inn. They do some simple pub food, though, so if you're in the village at lunchtime you'll be all right there."

"Worth our while adding the landlord to

the list of interviewees as well, given that the neighbour told us he saw Cunningham drinking in there even before he rented his cottage," remarked Haig.

"Agreed," replied Bryce, who was then silent for a minute. "We'll certainly need to see Mrs Cunningham ourselves, before long. In the meantime, Jephson's work today has cleared up a couple of potential leads – the telephone call to the office and the whereabouts of the car. But with nothing in the car, and no traceable information about the caller, neither takes us further forward."

Catchpole raised his eyebrows. "Isn't it worth getting the GPO to trace the telephone box, sir?"

Bryce shook his head. "If I was making a call that I didn't want traced – which after all, is a service known to the public – I wouldn't go to my local call box to do it. Anywhere but. Even if the man did use his local box, London is just a tad bigger than Ashton!

"No, my thoughts at the moment are going back to Allen again. I think you'd better arrange for some uniformed men to comb through that wood first thing tomorrow after all, Catchpole. If my thinking is correct, the gunman came across Allen in the wood, and that's where we'll find him, too."

The DI nodded and muttered something self-deprecating. "I probably should have found some manpower somehow and done it sooner myself, sir."

Bryce shook his head. "There are times when, with hindsight, every detective knows he's fallen short. But I don't believe this is one of them.

"Your budget constraints are very real, for a start. And I didn't think of Allen as a strong possibility for a victim earlier – not forgetting that your JP didn't, either. Taking a little holiday from home – which the son says his father does – is much more common than going missing in suspicious circumstances. Added to which, we already have three bodies. I haven't exactly jumped at the thought that we need to look for a fourth body now."

Catchpole was grateful for the Chief Inspector's fair-minded assessment. He took up his telephone and relayed the necessary search instructions. With his call concluded he said, "All done, sir, if you're ready to go? It's only a short distance to the Bull, and you can leave the car here, if you don't mind the walk with your bags?"

This was agreed, and Catchpole led the Yard detectives on foot to the hotel.

CHAPTER 6

The Bull was a large but unpretentious hostelry, with a slightly shabby but comfortable interior. A friendly greeting from the publican reassured the visiting detectives that they were welcome and would be looked after well.

"While we sign in and unload our bags, get yourself a drink and a pint of bitter each for Alex and me. Put everything on my tab," Bryce told the DI.

Noting Catchpole's surprise at the use of Haig's first name, he explained: "The opportunity didn't really arise the first time we met, but my policy has always been for informality when off duty. So tonight you are Trevor and this is Alex. I always offer for anyone to call me Philip, and you're welcome to do so, but few manage that, and most compromise on 'guv' instead. Just so long as there are no 'sirs'."

The local DI was even more surprised that Bryce knew his Christian name, although he vaguely thought he might have originally introduced himself as 'Trevor Catchpole' when they had worked together before. He went into the saloon bar and placed the order for the ales, taking a tray with the three pots to a quiet table at the far end of the room. He was enjoying his first gulp when the Chief Inspector joined him again.

"Alex is telephoning, Fiona, his wife. When he comes back I'll call Veronica."

"I hope Mrs Bryce is well, sir?"

"She is, yes, and I'll tell her I'm working with you again, Trevor. Vee will be pleased; for some reason she thought you were a good man."

"You'll need to put her right on that then, guv!" laughed the Inspector, nevertheless happy to have made a favourable first impression on a superior's wife.

Bryce took a long drink from his pint. "This bitter is good, and the rooms are pleasant – let's hope the food isn't a disappointment."

"I've never been here myself; I live in Ipswich and this is the first case I've been involved in around Woodbridge. But I hear it's good. One of my men was told to book you in here or the Crown, and apparently he spun a coin."

Haig joined them, and Bryce went off to the telephone. On his return, he found a handwritten menu card beside his beer glass, his companions having read it and discussed their choices. The trio gave their orders to a cheerful waitress, who spoke with a Suffolk accent even broader than that of Messrs Spraggons and Yarries. The detectives were very quickly taken into a small dining room and served soup, followed by faggots and mashed swede, the vegetable a perfect accompaniment to the hearty onion gravy in which the balls of minced liver, pork, and bacon, had been braised.

With their main course crockery cleared away, Catchpole explained what had been happening in the Felixstowe case as they waited for their chancellor's pudding to be served. Haig, who had played a crucial role while remaining in London, was as interested as his boss.

"It's been set down as the first case at the next Assizes – three weeks on Monday. I imagine you'll both get warning notices shortly. For the Crown, Finlay Aitchison is leading Robert Booth. Do you know them at all, guv?"

"Aitchison, yes – a superb advocate. I've heard very good things about Booth, but he's a few years younger than I am, and we've never met. Sounds like you have a strong team there."

The waitress delivered their desert and explained that the recipe was a variation on the original, dried fruits still being rationed and not always available.

"I see you've managed the cherries, though," said Bryce, "and a generous number, from the look of my portion."

"All from the little orchard out the back, sir. Picked and pipped in season. Not glacé as they ought to be of course, but set down in crocks with a bit of sugar and whatever nip of rum or brandy Mr Duffield can give the kitchen from the bar. We do apricots the same way. Honey to sweeten up the custard comes from the bee hives in the orchard, with the hens all pecking about in there as well, to give us the eggs for the custard."

She smiled, "And you won't be surprised nor shocked when I tell you that there's always some good but stale bread in a public house, on account of never knowing how much will be needed for our ploughman's each day."

She smiled again. "It mayn't be the proper recipe according to Mrs Beeton, but we've had customers tell us they think it's better; I believe you'll enjoy it!"

She was right.

***

A restful night and a well-cooked breakfast prepared the Yard officers for the day ahead as they took the short walk back to the police station the next morning. They found the DI had already arrived. Sitting in the little incident room, he was looking over his copies of the statements from London and the transcript of the reporter's notebook.

He rose as the DCI entered the room, but Bryce waved him down.

Catchpole had news. "I telephoned Allen's house as soon as I arrived. You were quite right – his son says he owns two shotguns. Only one of them in the house now.

"Men started searching the wood at eight

this morning, so they've been at it for half an hour. If they find anything, the Sergeant will use the call box in the village to contact us here. We may be in the village ourselves by then, depending on what you want to do."

"Haig and I will go to see the solicitors and Cunningham's colleagues at the newspaper offices," said the DCI. "Perhaps also his mother. Your work today, Catchpole, "is to see everyone whose name appears in Cunningham's notebook; I want preliminary interviews done with all of them, then we can decide who might need a follow-up. That's eleven people, all of them living in the village, as far as we know. Because Cunningham hasn't recorded anything of each conversation, I need to know what he asked, and what they told him. And I mean exactly what they told him – as near to word-for-word as they can remember.

"Is your DS coming here now, Catchpole?"

"Yes, sir; should arrive any minute."

"Good, you two make a start at talking to the eleven – as far as possible in the order that Cunningham recorded the names. We have no idea whether he approached everyone at random, or whether at some point in his questioning he selected his next interviewee based on what he'd just been told. Probably best to follow his footsteps as closely as we can. I suggest you take the notebook transcripts, such as they are, and make a show of checking what each of them says to you against Cunningham's notes of their conversation. It won't hurt for them to think that you already know everything there is to know about what they said – you just want to hear it from their own lips.

"You should also ask each person to whom he or she spoke after their conversation with Cunningham. Perhaps there were discussions in the Royal Oak, for example, or over the garden fence. It's just unfortunate that in the absence of anything helpful from Cunningham himself, we have to round up every possible scrap of information from every possible source."

"Yes, I get the idea, sir."

The jarring bell of the telephone interrupted Catchpole as he made his notes. He picked up the handset. The Yard detectives could hear an excited-sounding voice, followed by the Inspector's reply:

"Cordon off the body and don't touch it again. And don't touch the shotgun either. Leave two men on guard. I'll contact the police surgeon and get him over to Ashton. What's that? Very well, I'll come over now and break the news to the son. You and the rest of your men can resume normal duties."

The DI jiggled the receiver rest, and asked to be connected to the police surgeon. While waiting, he relayed what the uniformed officer had reported.

"As you've gathered, sir, they found a body in the woods. Constable Pyehurn lives in the next village, and knows Allen by sight; he's pretty sure it's him. Shotgun wounds to the chest again. A dead rabbit in his game bag and his gun lying beside him. It was broken, which as the Sergeant says couldn't have been done if the death had been suicide or accident."

Catchpole spoke briefly to the Doctor, arranging to meet him in the wood, and ended the call.

"You'll remember Doc Quilter, sir – our Police Surgeon for East Suffolk. He can't get to Ashton for an hour. But Jephson should be here any moment," said Catchpole, coming round the table and picking up his hat and overcoat, "so I'll be off. I'll call round and see Allen's son on the way – break the news and prepare him for the fact that he'll have to formally identify his father's body.

"If you're back and in the village by, say, one o'clock, sir, we could all have a bite to eat in the Royal Oak."

The Inspector departed, and Bryce and Haig talked over the morning's main event.

"Wrong place at the wrong time, poor man," said Haig.

"Yes. Perhaps he heard the shot which killed Wilcox, and wondered if his friend had got confused about whose day was whose, and went to investigate.

"Having said which, I've never heard a sawn-off gun fired, but I imagine the sound is distinguishable from that produced by a standard

12-bore. Maybe Allen realised it wasn't Wilcox's gun, and thought it was odd and went to see about it. All speculation, of course; I doubt we'll ever know what really happened."

Bryce stood up. "Let's go and talk to the people in Wilcox's old office, Sergeant, and see if we can come up with something concrete."

Haig took the wheel of the police Wolseley for the journey to Ipswich. As they passed the big RAF station at Martlesham Heath, Bryce told Haig to slow down, hoping to see the experimental Avro Lincoln bomber in which, according to rumour, the two outer Rolls Royce Merlin piston engines had been replaced by turboprops. Unfortunately, no aircraft of any sort were visible, and the Yard officers continued on their way.

Entering the town, with which neither man was familiar, Bryce navigated by means of the brief notes which the Desk Sergeant at Woodbridge had written for them. In a seedy street by the docks they passed a door, set in some very ornate but weathered arched brickwork, with two apparently octagonal uprights. Haig could see, even via the quick glance he spared the structure in passing, that this must once have been associated with a grand building, and made a comment. His boss, as ever, had some knowledge.

"You've just spotted something that my father told me about when he took me into the crypt at St Paul's Cathedral – it's Wolsey's Gate," he informed his Sergeant. "Turn right at the next junction, by the way.

"Cardinal Wolsey was born in Ipswich, and when he reached a certain level of wealth and influence he started to create a large college here, as a feeder establishment for Cardinal College at Oxford.

"Some of it was built by 1528, but then he fell out with Henry VIII, probably partly thanks to Anne Boleyn, who blamed Wolsey for not getting Henry's divorce sorted out quickly enough.

"Wolsey lost his position and power, and the buildings here were never completed. The King had the supplies of Caen stone and other materials that Wolsey had acquired for this project shipped to London, where they were used to finish York Palace – another of Wolsey's self-aggrandising ventures which the King had seized.

"Go left here, and we should come to Museum Street," advised Bryce, briefly interrupting himself to give Haig necessary directions.

"Cardinal College was also effectively seized by the King, and later renamed Christ Church."

"I knew that Wolsey was a great planner and builder, sir." said Haig, "and that Hampton Court was originally his; but as I recall, he handed that over to the King more or less voluntarily. What I don't understand..." Haig concentrated on making the turn "...is how the doorway we've just seen and his other grand buildings tie in with St Paul's – I definitely know he didn't build that!"

"The connection is one of his lesser-known plans – in this case for his own funeral. He had a sarcophagus made from black marble, and after his downfall Henry grabbed that too, apparently intending to have himself interred in it. For some reason that never happened, and the thing lay in storage for nearly three hundred years. Eventually it was used for the body of Admiral Nelson, now in the crypt of St Paul's.

"As my father told me, if all had gone according to Wolsey's plan, it would have been his cardinal's hat resting on the sarcophagus, and not the viscount's coronet that we see today.

"Ah, here's our destination – park wherever you can, Sergeant.

The detectives pushed open the street door of *Purdue, Parsons, Congreve & Wilcox* and entered the spacious reception. Three clients were seated in comfortable armchairs waiting for their appointments, with a fourth standing by an old carved buffet, inspecting the periodicals and papers spread out on its polished surface. Bryce thought what a sensible alternative use this was for the distinguished item of furniture, which looked every bit as handsome covered in magazines, instead of the more usual breakfast dishes which such a piece was designed to hold.

Sergeant Haig discreetly explained to the receptionist who they were and what they wanted.

The girl was quick-witted, and also lowered her voice so that she couldn't be overheard. "Oh yes, I see, sir, I'll tell our senior partner that you're here; his first appointment hasn't arrived yet, so he doesn't have anyone with him at the moment." She stood and quickly ran up the staircase and out of sight.

In less than a minute she returned, accompanied by a thickset man with very little hair and wearing spectacles with extremely thick lenses.

"Duncan Congreve, gentlemen, senior partner here. Let me show you to my office." To the receptionist he said, "Katharine, be an angel please, and rustle up three coffees."

The detectives had visited several provincial solicitors in the course of their duties, and had almost invariably found that they did very well for themselves. It was abundantly clear that Congreve ran a profitable business; the office they were led into could only be described as sumptuous.

The Solicitor invited the policemen to take easy chairs beside a low table. "Terrible thing about poor George," he said. "Such a shock. I had a local reporter asking questions recently, and in fact I've agreed to see him tomorrow." A sudden thought occurred to Congreve. "I trust that my speaking to him won't interfere with your investigation in any way?"

Bryce shook his head. "It won't because it can't," he replied. "I'm afraid that the reporter, Marcus Cunningham, has also been shot dead; at Liverpool Street station the night before last. That news should have made the national papers this morning, if not the regionals. Another Ashton resident has also been killed."

The lawyer stared at the DCI, his eyes and mouth wide open in surprise. Before he could speak again there was a tap on the door, and the receptionist arrived with a tray. Congreve questioned her as she handed out the cups and set down a biscuit plate. "Have Riddell's delivered the papers today?"

"Not yet, Mr Congreve. They get later and later," complained the girl.

"Bring the *Times* and the *Telegraph* up to me as soon as they arrive, Katharine, thank you."

With the door closed, Congreve explained that he didn't have a morning paper delivered to his home, as nothing ruined his breakfast more completely or gave him indigestion more quickly than the endless round of political news. "Well, I've certainly grasped why Scotland Yard is involved," he said. "Do I take it that the shooting of the reporter is somehow linked to this other death – and George's?"

"That's the line we're working on," agreed Bryce. "All three were killed with shotguns, and at least two of those – George Wilcox and Marcus Cunningham – were with an illegally sawn-off weapon. We expect to find the same is true for the third victim."

Congreve's expression of astonishment was replaced with one of horror. "A sawn-off shotgun?

Again? I could scarcely believe it when we learned that was how poor George was killed – and now you're suggesting two more victims met the same end. It's the sort of thing that happens in Chicago – not Suffolk! Not even in Liverpool Street, come to that."

Bryce nodded. "Pretty much what Sergeant Haig here, said, wondering if the gunman might be a foreigner – perhaps an American. We haven't identified the man yet. He's dead too, by the way; shot at Liverpool Street. Best thing to happen, in many ways – although it does mean we can never question him. As you can appreciate, that lost opportunity inevitably slows us down. But we assume the gunman was commissioned to kill Mr Wilcox and Mr Cunningham, and it's obviously the paymaster we need to find now.

"Anyway, your former colleague was the first to die, and we need to know why. It's imperative we establish the motive for his killing; once we have the key to that, we can unlock the subsequent shootings. So, can you think of anyone with anything against Mr Wilcox – either professionally, or in his private life?"

Congreve was at a loss. "No, Chief Inspector, I can't. And it seems you perhaps don't know that George and I weren't just colleagues. He was also my brother-in-law; it was I who introduced him to my older sister, Hermione, soon after he joined the firm.

"It was a late marriage for both of them, and

they had no children. After Hermione died, George withdrew a bit, and I confess I was surprised when he decided to retire. With Hermione gone, I should have thought he would want to keep the structure and mental discipline of work – I know I would, were I in his position. But that was his choice, and when I saw him a fortnight ago I didn't think there was anything amiss with him. A little more subdued, perhaps; but no more than that.

"As for the business side of things, he'd been a partner in this firm for almost twenty years, taking over when old Jasper Parsons died. George dealt only with wills and probate matters."

Congreve drank some coffee. "Very few court appearances in that field, so a dearth of clients who might have felt hard done by after losing a case. He never handled civil claims of any other sort, and no criminal work.

The Solicitor's eyes narrowed as he frowned. "I do recall there was a case about five years ago," he said slowly, "where a client wanted to contest a will. A valuable estate, too. Now that was a matter George was instructed to take all the way to court, and our client succeeded in getting the original dispositions altered partly in her favour. She was obviously very happy with him. But not so the original legatee, who by all accounts was furious, even though he was still left with a substantial sum."

Congreve, having supplied this example of possible motive as required, emphasised his next point heavily, looking and sounding bewildered as he did so. "But it's all such a long time ago. Surely, Chief Inspector, people don't brood and fester almost indefinitely before *doing* anything?"

Bryce treated the question as rhetorical, and made no response.

The Solicitor continued, "You'll need to speak to someone else in the firm to get the specifics about that matter. If you've finished your coffee, gentlemen, I'll take you in to see Colin Jago now. He used to assist George and will step into his shoes to take on the partnership. And I'm sure Cecily Botwright, who used to be George's secretary, would know – or could dig out – the details about that court case."

Congreve stood up as he spoke and extended his hand to Bryce and Haig, "See you get this murderer, please gentlemen," he said, and led the way to his colleague's office.

Mr Jago's room was not quite so well appointed as the senior partner's, but was still large and well-furnished. It's occupant was middle-aged, short, and with a beard in the style of Field Marshal Smuts. He stood up in surprise as his senior led the two detectives into his office. "I was expecting Sir Malcolm and Lady Wrotham," he said.

"This is rather more important, Colin," Congreve told him, and performed the introductions. "I'll fetch the Wrothams and entertain them in my office until you're ready." He excused himself, remarking that he'd be glad to answer any further questions which the officers might think of later.

"Most dreadful business about George," Jago said, as the three men sat down. "Mistaken identity, perhaps? Or accident?"

"No to both, Mr Jago," said Bryce, and gave the lawyer all the necessary details.

"Good Lord!" exclaimed Jago. "I did read something in the paper today about a madman in London – but I had no idea it was connected with poor George."

"So you don't know of anyone who might want to kill your late colleague?"

Jago shook his head. "I most certainly don't. It's beyond understanding that anyone would have reason to kill him."

"What do you know about a probate case of a few years ago, in which your firm's client claimed an entitlement to part of a large estate, and succeeded in that claim?"

"That must have been four or more years ago. I wasn't involved directly, but I heard about it, naturally." Jago shook his head again. "I can't be of any real help to you regarding that case, but I'll go and find Mrs Botwright." He stood up. "I guarantee she'll have the facts in her head – she has the most exceptional memory," he added over his shoulder as he left the room.

A minute later, Bryce and Haig rose to their feet as Jago returned with a smartly dressed woman. Nearer to fifty than forty, she was expensively dressed, with some tasteful jewellery displayed on her fingers and the lapel of her costume jacket. Bryce thought she might easily be taken for the wife of a prosperous consultant surgeon or similarly well-paid professional, rather than a secretary. Jago performed the introductions and Haig gave the secretary a brief outline of the four deaths.

Mrs Botwright was remarkably sanguine. "My goodness," she said, calmly, "bad enough to hear about poor Mr Wilcox; but two other murders on top! Still, it's good the killer got what he deserved.

"Mr Jago tells me you're interested in a contested will case Mr Wilcox handled – Orbell and Mytton.

"Yes, it's essential that we find the motive for killing Mr Wilcox and it's just possible that case may be relevant. What can you tell us?

"Quite a lot, actually, Chief Inspector. It all came to a head a few months after the end of the war. Our client was Miss Patience Orbell. She'd been brought up by her mother and stepfather, her own father having died unexpectedly in 1927, shortly after she was born. The next year, her mother married Mr Mytton. He was a widower, also with one child who was several years older than Patience.

"The new Mrs Mytton – who had little money of her own – died towards the end of the war, and the stepfather followed a matter of weeks afterwards – both of them rather prematurely, I may say. Mytton's estate was valued for probate at something approaching a quarter of a million pounds. His will left everything to his son Tobias – Miss Orbell's stepbrother.

"Patience came in to consult Mr Wilcox, with a view to disputing the will. I sat in on the original meeting to take notes.

"Mr Wilcox thought she had a compelling case. She was only eighteen, so still a minor, but there was no arrangement for her guardianship in either her mother's or her stepfather's wills. However, she had been dependent on Mytton almost her entire life. Her mother had of course been Mytton's wife for that period too – and stepmother to Tobias, helping to bring him up.

"Mr Wilcox took advice from Sebastian Landor, specialist counsel in London. Mr Landor agreed there was a good case, and suggested that in the first instance Mr Wilcox should negotiate with the son."

"Without any joy, I take it?" asked Bryce.

"Quite right," replied Mrs Botwright. "Tobias Mytton refused even to discuss the matter.

"Everything progressed to the High Court, where the judge set aside the original will, and awarded thirty percent of the estate to Miss Orbell. Because Mytton had been so obdurate about a settlement, the judge ordered him to pay Miss Orbell's costs in their entirety, too. You perhaps wouldn't know, Chief Inspector, but that isn't very usual at all."

Haig wasn't surprised that the DCI didn't point out that he did know this, nor declare his own legal qualifications. The Sergeant had observed that his boss was disinclined to reveal his credentials unless it served a useful purpose to do so.

"Mr Wilcox was in court, of course," continued the secretary. "He said Tobias Mytton was livid. As soon as the judge retired, Mytton began to rant at his barrister, and shouted across the courtroom at Mr Landor and Mr Wilcox, apparently.

"But as far as Mr Wilcox was concerned, that was the end of the matter. He was just happy for his client. And I can tell you that in all the years afterwards he never once suggested to me that Mytton had contacted him, or repeated his outburst. I feel sure he would have done so, had it happened," the secretary concluded, before thinking to add, "but if you need to contact Miss Orbell, I can find her last-known address. Naturally, she may have moved on or got married since then, but it would be a starting point for you. We have all the old details for Tobias Mytton, as well."

With nothing further to be learned about a possible motive, Bryce thanked Jago and Mrs Botwright for their help, and said the detectives would wait downstairs for the promised addresses.

Back on the ground floor, Bryce asked the receptionist for directions to the offices of the *Anglian Examiner* as Haig thumbed through a magazine on the buffet.

Minutes later, the Yard officers had everything they needed and returned to their car in Museum Street.

"What do you think of this Mytton thing, sir?" asked Haig from behind the wheel of the Wolseley.

Bryce grunted. "After such a long time, it seems unlikely in the extreme – as all three of those we've just spoken to agree. However, it's the only thing we know about where anyone had any reason to dislike Wilcox."

"Aye. But from what we've just learned, Miss Orbell's thirty percent left young Mytton with the best part of a hundred and seventy-five thousand, sir. Me, even if I still didn't choose to acknowledge my stepsister's right to some of the cash, I'd have just sworn a bit and then gone away to enjoy the rest of my life in comfort."

"Me too, Sergeant. But maybe we're just a pair of fair-minded and generous types! No, Tobias Mytton definitely needs looking at, but that can be a job for Catchpole and Jephson.

"Let's see who we can find at the newspaper offices."

They found the *Examiner* headquarters without difficulty. Inside, the receptionist was rather more emotional than the solicitors' receptionist had been, her eyes instantly welling up at the mention of the deceased reporter's name.

"Oh yes, gentlemen," she sniffed, "poor Marcus. Best person for you to talk to is Neville Dearden. He sat closest to Marcus in the office. They were friends. I know he's in – I'll just see if he's free."

The girl disappeared through a door behind her. Returning within a minute, she was accompanied by a young man in his mid-twenties with an untidy head of brown hair and a small moustache of similar colour. This facial hair may have been intended to give him a more mature look, but the sparseness of growth rather undid the effect.

"Come and have a seat, gents," said the young journalist pleasantly, as he led the detectives to a small room in the corner of the main office. "Scotland Yard, no less! Glad to see that the local police are getting the experts in on this thoroughly nasty business. What would you like to ask me?"

"I'm not sure how much you know, Mr Dearden; the Sergeant here will give you the outline."

Dearden sat silently throughout Haig's report.

"I see," he said. "Presumably you believe that Marcus was on to something and had to be removed. The question being, I suppose: what was it that Marcus found out – and do I know anything about it?"

"Very well put," said Bryce, approving Dearden's swift grasp of his own possible importance to the investigation. "Yes, that's it in a nutshell."

"Did Mr Cunningham confide in you regarding this case?" asked Haig, his pencil ready to record everything the reporter said.

"Unfortunately not. And given that this would be the scoop of the century for me and the *Examiner*, it's a pity that I'm in the dark about it all." The young man sat back in his seat, his Adam's apple bobbing as he swallowed hard. Clearly upset, he said in a breaking voice, "But much more than that, I'm desperately, desperately sorry about Marcus. I want to see whoever is responsible at the end of a rope."

He shook out a handkerchief and blew his nose. "We were good friends, the two of us, but you have to understand he was a complete oyster when it came to following leads. Which was fair enough, of course – we were rivals in a sense, and I'd already got in ahead of him on a couple of occasions for some juicy titbits. Marcus was chafing to scoop something really significant himself."

"What do you know about his property in Ashton – how long had he been there, for instance?"

"All I know is that about four months ago he was scouting around to rent something there.

After he first said that was his intention, I don't recall he ever spoke of it again. If I had to guess his reason, and I feel a complete brute for saying it, I think it was probably to dodge his widowed mother from time to time.

"He came from a well-fixed family, you know; not hugely wealthy, but no wolves at their door. He was the youngest of three boys and was still living at home. Actually, he was the only son still living; his brothers were both lost in the war. I think he found his mother..." Dearden again sounded torn as to whether he should speak his mind, before spitting out his opinion. "Look, this will sound an awful thing to say about a woman who's just lost her last son, but I think he found her overwhelming, actually. I got the impression that she was especially intrusive when it came to girlfriends, and managed to scare off at least one that Marcus particularly liked, pushing at her the idea of early marriage and a large brood of children."

Sergeant Haig nodded understandingly. "You mean pretty off-putting for any girl to feel that her future mother-in-law will control her married life."

"Precisely. I wouldn't be surprised if he just wanted somewhere to get a bit of peace and privacy sometimes.

"I've gone through his desk, and you're more than welcome to take a look yourselves. As I expected, there was nothing of interest; I found a few old notebooks and couple of unused ones, a supply of pencils, and all the usual desk detritus – nothing more."

The young journalist sat forward. "But what about his current notebook, Chief Inspector; that would surely be far more interesting for you. Do you have it?"

"We do, yes, and someone has managed to translate it for us. It's of interest, as it mentions interviews he had with people in his village, after Wilcox's death."

Dearden smiled. "I like your tactful 'managed to translate'. Marcus was a bit sloppy with his Pitman's. Still, it was only for himself."

Bryce rose. "If that's all you can tell us, Mr Dearden, we'll be on our way."

"I don't suppose you'd like to give me a statement before you go, Chief Inspector?" asked the reporter eagerly.

"Not at this stage, no. But you already have more information than any other journalist, because nothing has been said to link Cunningham's death in London with the murder of Wilcox or Allen. I have no objection to your using all of that. You have a head start!"

The Yard officers were soon back in their car.

"I think we'll skip seeing the mother for the moment," said Bryce. "Between Jephson's report yesterday and what we've just been told by Dearden, it sounds like that lady has had a great deal of additional grief put on her. We'll allow her a little more time to recover.

"Head back to Ashton instead, Sergeant, and we'll get some lunch."

CHAPTER 7

The Yard detectives saw Catchpole's car parked beside the green, and Haig pulled up behind it. There was no sign of the Suffolk policemen, and as it was still only a quarter to one the DCI suggested they amble around for a few minutes, until the local detectives appeared for their mid-day break.

It was good walking weather, with a bright blue sky and a low hanging sun; and whilst not warm, when standing in the sunshine it was very pleasant.

Arriving at the village church, they stopped to look at the ancient lychgate. Both mentally compared it to the one they had seen and discussed recently when on a case in Oxfordshire. Admiring the church, with its round tower topped by an octagonal belfry, Bryce was tempted to go and look inside. That decision was forestalled, however, as a beaming priest hurried along the footpath towards them, cassock flapping beneath his overcoat. The cleric stopped when he reached the detectives.

"Good afternoon, gentlemen – welcome

to the church of St Barnabas. I'm Gregory Mickleburgh, Vicar of this parish. You look, forgive me if I'm wrong, like policemen."

Bryce, knowing that the local Vicar was on the list of eleven to be interviewed, returned the cleric's jovial smile and introduced himself and Haig, before enquiring whether Mickleburgh had already been seen by the Ipswich detectives.

"Ah," said the Vicar, "so a superior force has been called in. No, I've not spoken to anyone today apart from Mrs Tippett, who does our flowers. It was she who told me about our occasionally-resident journalist, and she says there is a rumour that poor Desmond Allen is dead too."

The Reverend Mickleburgh suddenly transmogrified, and thrust a forefinger upwards to the heavens. In a thunderous voice he shouted "Beelzebub and his minions are in our presence! Mark my words; Satan has been at work here – this village is cursed with his evil doings! Cursed, I tell you!"

Bryce, taken aback by this extraordinary change from initial approachability to fire and brimstone fury, quickly responded with the facts of the matter.

"With respect, Vicar, I doubt that's true. Someone came to Ashton, apparently to murder George Wilcox. Whilst here, they may have killed another villager, probably to avoid being identified.

"We don't yet know why Mr Wilcox was

killed, but one can reasonably assume that wherever he lived, the outcome would have been the same. Your village is no more cursed than any other."

Mickleburgh transformed again. He now became the admonishing parent, giving necessary correction to a challenging child who had missed the crucial and self-evident point of a previous lesson.

"Naturally, you speak as a representative of man's laws, Chief Inspector," he said. "But I am a man of God, charged to look out for the devil's works. I can assure you they are to be found everywhere and in everything." He stared straight into the Chief Inspector's grey eyes, "And they are to be found in everyone, I tell you! Everyone!"

Bryce decided it was time to change the subject. "Your church, Vicar – we hardly have time to view it today, but would I be right in thinking its unusual tower dates to the 13th century?"

The cleric immediately reverted to his earlier warmth of manner. "Oh indeed, yes. With some later additions as is invariably the case with these ecclesiastical buildings. The tower is certainly unusual, but not unique. St Andrew's in Hasketon, not five miles away, has a very similar one."

"If you'll permit my asking work questions out here, Vicar, can you tell us anything about Mr Wilcox?"

Mickleburgh nodded. "I knew him quite

well. I've been the incumbent here for eight years, and George had lived in the village for a good few years before that. He was a member of the Parochial Church Council when I arrived, and only resigned after the sad death of his wife – a very devout lady. He often read a lesson at Matins, but he didn't keep that up either, after he was widowed.

"They were keen on our whist drives, Hermione and George, and they were also members of a little set of bridge players who host bridge evenings in their homes. He dropped out of those not long after she died, even though there was always another partner available.

"I don't know what others have told the police, but I have to admit that George didn't suffer fools gladly. When playing bridge, for example, he could be very rude to his partner if he or she made an error.

"Also, the PCC has some members who are, shall we say, not quite so intellectually able as others. There were a few occasions when George, having failed to persuade someone on a point, resorted to shouting – as though volume of voice was a substitute for logical argument.

"But it's over a year since there was such an incident. And anyway, I hardly think any of those involved took serious umbrage even at the time."

"Thank you. It's always important for the police to learn about all facets of a victim, when trying to establish motive for a crime," said the

DCI.

"By the way, sir," interjected Haig, "Inspector Catchpole has been speaking to the villagers mentioned in Mr Cunningham's notebook. Our theory, as you will appreciate, is that one or more of those interviews caused the murderer concern, to such an extent that he then killed the reporter – or ordered his killing."

"Ah yes, I see, Sergeant. I wasn't thinking of what I believe is called a contract killing – I just assumed the murderer wanted to kill George, for whatever reason. Now I see that is probably wrong. Oh dear, oh dear."

Haig pressed his point. "So do you know of any other incidents, outside the card table and the PCC?"

The priest became reticent. "I only mentioned those examples because I felt you shouldn't go away with the notion that George was perfect in every way. Of course he wasn't – none of us is. The PCC incidents, and occasional flashes of rudeness at the bridge table, I saw and heard myself. Anything else is hearsay, which I'm not prepared to repeat.

"All I will say is this: you could try Vincent Eddington, who owns the land behind George's house, and is the freeholder of Mr Cunningham's cottage in The Old Loke. He's not local; he lives miles away in Woolpit."

The Vicar's reluctance was now even more visible, but he gave up a little more information for

Haig to record. "And perhaps some time spent with Christina Fielding and Cynthia Redfern, both in the village here, might be time well spent for you.

"Now, if you'll excuse me, I'm late for lunch, and my wife will scold me if it gets spoiled. Do come back and look inside the church when you have time. Good day to you both."

The Vicar moved away at speed and the Yard detectives, turning back towards the Royal Oak, saw Catchpole and his colleague approaching. The four men met by the pub door. Bryce, who had briefly met DS Jephson before, introduced Haig, who was not only of similar age, but shared his opposite number's short and stocky build.

Inside, the only food available was ham sandwiches, but when these appeared the four officers were not disappointed. The bread was decently buttered and the dry cured ham a fair thickness and very tasty. Each plate carried two large pickled onions and a pickled egg. With a half-pint of bitter to wash down the meal, no one was dissatisfied.

Apart from themselves, the saloon bar was nearly empty, and nobody was within earshot of the corner table at which the policemen sat. They had so far not seen the landlord, and when the coffee was delivered to their table Bryce asked the waitress if the publican was available, thinking that an interview with that gentleman could be conveniently arranged whilst they were in the pub.

"Oh no, sir. Mr Sanderson won't be back

until this evening," the girl told him with a smile. "Alternate Mondays are his day for horse trading, as he calls it. He goes into town and gets in all the essentials for us." She bobbed her head and left.

The conversation turned to the morning's work.

"Fill everyone in about our visits to the solicitor's office and the newspaper, Sergeant," said Bryce.

Haig gave his report.

"As you've just heard, very little for us in all that," said the Chief Inspector. "It really doesn't seem likely that after all these years this business with Mytton can be relevant. Nevertheless, you and Sergeant Jephson must go and see him, Inspector.

"Has the younger Allen seen the body now?"

"Yes, sir," replied Catchpole. "He identified his father. Quite steady he was, under the circumstances – the wound was very off-putting. He also showed us the shotgun certificate, and one of the numbers matched the gun found by the body. No doubt at all about identity.

"Doc Quilter has been. Provisionally, he thinks Allen wasn't shot at such a close range as Wilcox. There didn't seem to be many pellets entering the chest. I told him your expert is going to do some test firing of what we assume is the murder weapon, and he said that would help to determine the range – if that becomes relevant. He'll do the PM this evening, sir, and get the report to Woodbridge by ten o'clock tomorrow."

"Good. What about your interviews this morning?"

Catchpole motioned to Jephson to report. It was almost the first time Bryce had heard the DS say more than a couple of words, but he wasn't surprised to hear a deep Suffolk burr, not much less marked that that of old Mr Spraggons.

"We've spoken to seven of the village people that Mr Cunningham had notes on, sir. Can't say that anything new came out of it. They all said he'd asked them about what Mr Wilcox was like; whether anyone had arguments or disputes with him; whether he was popular.

"The ones we spoke to this morning said they knew nothing against him at all. But it happened that our seven are all from the working classes, sir. They'd no professional truck with him and no close social contact either; just a 'how do' and the usual time-of-day greetings whenever they saw him.

"All of them said they'd talked to other people about their conversations with Cunningham, and about the case in general. Three of them mentioned discussions in here, when apparently several people were together and chatting while they were supping."

"Did anyone mention the fact that Wilcox had a short fuse?" asked Haig.

"Well, one young chap said Wilcox'd been known to shout a bit if he was annoyed," replied

Jephson, "but the lad couldn't give us an actual example."

"We bumped into the Vicar a few minutes ago," said Bryce. "He told us he hadn't spoken to you yet, so we had a chat with him." The DCI recounted the conversation.

"However, he did suggest we should talk to three people in particular. Christina Fielding is on our list already, of course. But he also suggests Vincent Eddington – the owner of both the woodland and Cunningham's cottage – and a Cynthia Redfern. From what you say, you haven't interviewed Mrs Fielding yet?"

"No sir. She's on the list for this afternoon. We've heard no mention of a Mrs Redfern, and we've only heard Eddington mentioned in connection with the shooting rights."

Jephson put a tick beside the Vicar in his notebook, and added the names of Redfern and Eddington. Catchpole continued:

"Now you've spoken to the Reverend, we've ticked off eight between us. There's only Mrs Fielding, and two others left from the list – the sub-postmistress and the doctor's wife."

Bryce nodded in acknowledgement, and proceeded to set out what needed to be accomplished that afternoon.

"Inspector, I want you and Sergeant Jephson to go and see Eddington. He lives miles away in Woolpit, and you two know how to get about the county better than we do.

"Push him as much as necessary. The Vicar was so circumspect that I don't believe he would mention the name at all without good reason – there's something to learn there.

"If you come back via Stowmarket you can call on Tobias Mytton; Haig has his address for you. I can't say I expect anything useful from him," continued Bryce, "but we must be thorough.

"We didn't see Mrs Cunningham this morning. As you come back through Ipswich, go and see her. Make quite sure her son said nothing to her about his murder enquiries, and see if she can shed any more light on why he took his cottage in Ashton. It may just be a coincidence, but it seems a funny sort of place to pick for someone who, according to his pal at the paper, came from a comfortably-off background."

With the last swallow of his coffee, Bryce announced that he and Haig would take over the interviews for the remaining villagers on the list, and also locate the newly-mentioned Cynthia Redfern."

Catchpole stood up. "There's a telephone in the bar here. I'll try and contact Eddington and tell him to expect us, before we go all the way out to Woolpit."

"Good idea," said Bryce. "When you've finished let me know; I want to talk to the Yard."

***

Bryce went to pay at the bar, while Catchpole

asked the operator to find a number for Eddington, Woolpit being outside the local telephone directory's area.

"I'm looking for a Cynthia Redfern – can you help me?" the DCI asked the barmaid, when he had settled the bill. Expecting a brief response, he was delighted to receive a fulsome reply.

"Oh yes, sir. She's the Lady of the Manor, really, since the Squire died a while back. The Redferns have been here for hundreds of years. Although Mr Eddington owns a fair bit of land and properties hereabouts, I reckon Mrs Redfern has more. She lives at Ashton Hall. That's in the parish but not really in the village. Go out on the road towards Woodbridge from here and take the first turning left. You can't miss the gates on the right-hand side – not a quarter mile past the last house, I'd say."

Thanking the woman, Bryce picked up the telephone which Catchpole, giving the DCI a 'thumbs up' sign, had just put down.

After some delay, contact was made with Scotland Yard. First, Bryce spoke to his secretary. That conversation was quickly concluded and produced no new information. He then asked to be transferred to the CID office, where Barker was at his desk.

"Hello sir," started the detective constable, "did you get my message?"

"No. I'm in the middle of nowhere and haven't been back to the station. What have you got?"

"A probable identification, sir!" Barker sounded excited. "Inspector Bygraves called from Islington. One of his men was showing the photo around in his patch and struck lucky. A local nark – name of Stanley Sims – recognised the shooter. He needed a lot of assurance that the gunman was really dead, but eventually he came up with a name: Abe Dean. The squeaker reckons he was from America."

Bryce grinned to himself. Haig might have been right all along.

"Sims had heard that if anyone wanted someone 'rubbed out', Dean would do it for a price. He reckoned the going rate was seven hundred and fifty pounds. Said he didn't know where the man lived. But he told the copper to ask around a pub called The Feathers – a dreadful dive, by all accounts. Sims reckoned that's where potential clients could make contact.

"Mr Bygraves went to the pub with a bit of back-up. Asked a few questions, and took the landlord and another chap to the station.

"Soon as the pair heard Dean was dead, there was a lot of squealing. They got an address. The landlord said that Dean rarely ventured outside – he'd only seen him twice. He suggested Dean was here illegally, possibly a US army deserter. That's being looked into.

"The landlord claimed to know nothing of Dean's trade. He reckons all he did was send a boy round with any message left at the bar. What happened after that wasn't his affair, so far as he was concerned. But Mr Bygraves took a different view, and he's being held on suspicion of being an accessory to murder.

"The Islington boys are applying for a warrant as we speak, sir, and I'm about to leave to join them on the raid. Just in case there's anyone else on the premises to object, Mr Bygraves thinks going in 'mob-handed' is a wise precaution."

"Excellent, Barker, that's all very good news."

"Just one other thing, sir; the Armourer would appreciate a word. Shall I get your call transferred?"

"Yes, do that please. Then go and do your bit with the Islington crowd."

A few seconds later, Inspector Bailey came on the line. Is that you, Philip?"

"Yes; hello Freddie, what have you got on the Sauer?"

"Not a lot. Your man loaded his own cartridges. I don't know how he obtained his supplies, but I understand from Barker that they're searching his premises this afternoon, so perhaps we'll see what equipment he used. The cartridges are very well made, so regardless of anything else the man was a professional in that sense alone.

"He is also the most appalling vandal, of course. Bad enough to chop down the barrel of any old shotgun, but to ruin a rare quality piece like an M30 is arguably even worse than doing it to a

Purdey or a Holland and Holland."

"I'd never seen an M30 before," remarked Bryce.

"Nor had I," replied Bailey. "I'm hoping I can keep this one for our little museum of specials. Pity it's not intact, but still…

"Anyway, you provided ten cartridges. I opened two up, to see the loading and so on. Both had six LG pellets. I test-fired a further six – two at each of three distances. I'll let you have the detailed results. Suffice it to say that even if anyone was lunatic enough to use LG shot for small game, you certainly wouldn't use this gun to go after pheasants or rabbits with these cartridges. At twenty-five yards not a single pellet hit my target – which is a bit bigger than a rabbit!

"No ammunition for the rifle, although if we could get some I'd like to try that for accuracy as well. I've never come across a sawn-off rifle before!"

Bryce thanked his friend, and replaced the handset.

CHAPTER 8

"I doubt you gathered any of that," said Bryce to his Sergeant outside the pub and out of earshot of anyone else, "because I didn't want to repeat anything of the conversation as I usually would. The gunman may well be an American, as you thought, and he has a name – Abe Dean – although I suppose that may not be genuine." The DCI gave an outline of everything else he had learned.

Haig whistled when he heard the alleged fee charged for a murder.

"Not many could afford those rates, sir. If this was a contract killing, we're not looking for some poor Suffolk peasant!"

"No, indeed," replied the DCI thoughtfully. "And, unless Dean offered a discount for quantity, that probably means someone would have handed over fifteen hundred pounds, presumably before both jobs were done. I think we can assume that there wasn't a charge for Allen's death.

"I sometimes dip into Whitaker's Almanac," continued the Chief Inspector, "it provides some interesting figures about public salaries. Just to put the contract price into perspective, our Assistant Commissioner could afford a couple of fees if he spent almost his entire annual salary – but the director of the Hendon lab couldn't!"

Haig laughed. "I don't suppose Whitaker's goes down to my humble level, but it'd take me many years of saving!"

Bryce consulted the names on Catchpole's list.

"Mrs Fielding is next – Strickland House, Woodbridge Road."

They looked around the green. Ashton was one of those villages where a relief postman would have great difficulty – there were no house numbers, only names. But at least Woodbridge Road was easy enough to identify, being the main road through the village. They were fortunate – the second house past the green was a substantial three-storey property built in grey stone, with the name clearly marked.

The front door was equipped with a pull-handle for the bell. Haig gave this a good tug, and a deep clanging could be heard inside. A few seconds later, a neatly-uniformed maid opened the door. Bryce explained who they were, and asked to see the lady of the house.

The maid looked apprehensive, and appeared to consider asking them to wait on the step before reconsidering, perhaps swayed by Bryce's pleasant and refined accent, and inviting them inside.

"If you wait in the parlour, gentlemen, I'll see if the mistress is available."

"Oh, I think she will be, young lady," said the DCI, "when you tell her this is a murder investigation, not a social call."

The maid quickly backed out of the room, shutting the door behind her.

The detectives took in their surroundings as they waited. The room was large and well-proportioned, a curved bay window to the front allowing plenty of natural light to illuminate the interior even though the fine morning had turned into a dull afternoon. Solid English oak furniture, with chintz soft furnishings and drapery, combined to make a welcoming place to relax.

Leaving Haig warming himself by the fire and admiring the mantlepiece, Bryce wandered towards the end of the room, where a dozen or so paintings of various sizes were grouped together on a wall, in an eye-catching arrangement. He took a closer look. All were landscapes, carefully executed and exquisitely detailed in vibrant oil colours. His attention was particularly held by two of the paintings which captured the vividness of a summer's day on a shore, and a misty sunrise in a valley.

The door opened and Mrs Fielding entered. As the Yard detectives had noted earlier, she was a well-built and striking woman, with black eyes and greying black hair. The tailored skirt and jacket she wore perfectly suited her upright posture. Her rather sallow complexion, however, was not at all complimented by her heavily applied coral lipstick.

"I hadn't expected to see you again so soon," she said, "do please sit down. It's not long after lunch, gentlemen, but would you care for any refreshments?"

Bryce thanked her and declined. "I was admiring your beautiful paintings, Mrs Fielding," he said as he sat down. "One of the locations feels familiar to me – I feel as if I might have been there myself."

"They're all somewhere in Wales, Chief Inspector. You've obviously been to those beautiful places," said his hostess in surprised delight. "I must say I've no idea where my late husband acquired them; they were already in his possession when I married him. He was very fond of them and would often stand where you stood, gazing at them and remembering his youth in one of his favourite parts of the world."

Bryce returned her smile and broached the first of his questions.

"This morning, our two Suffolk colleagues called on some of the people who were interviewed by the late Mr Cunningham; the Sergeant and I are now visiting the remainder.

"As I said to your little group yesterday, it's quite certain that the murderer became worried about the reporter's questions, and took drastic steps to silence him. Whether he – or she – spoke to

Mr Cunningham personally, or only got to hear via a third party, we don't yet know.

"We have Mr Cunningham's shorthand notes, of course, but it would be helpful if you can tell us what questions he put to you, and what you replied. As near as possible to the original, if you would. Then we need to know who, if anyone, you discussed this with."

Mrs Fielding nodded. "I think I can remember accurately enough, because he only asked a few questions, Chief Inspector. Let me see. 'Do you know anyone with cause to kill George Wilcox?' 'For how long had you known him?' 'How well did you know him?'"

The lady of the house knitted her black eyebrows together and dredged up one more of the reporter's questions. 'What sort of man was he?' He did also ask something about George's old firm, but I knew nothing about that."

"As for my answers, well, I wasn't best pleased at being accosted – this was in public outside the village shop, you understand, and he was quite thrusting and determined in his manner. But as far as I recall, all I was able to tell him was that I'd known George ever since he and his wife moved here, twenty or so years ago. I knew him quite well. I've lived in this village for twenty-five years. I came with my first husband, who died in 1929; I subsequently remarried.

"After George and Hermione moved here, we saw a lot of them. Before my second husband died and George's wife died – in quick succession about eighteen months ago – we used to play bridge and whist regularly, and often met for tea or supper in each other's house. Or in other houses – the vicarage, for example." She smiled. "The Vicar is very keen on his cards, despite all his 'work of the devil' denunciations!"

Haig smiled at Mrs Fielding's remark, confirming as it did that the Vicar's earlier display was not an isolated one. "Aye, we've met your padre – I imagine Sunday sermons can get quite lively," he said.

"That's an understatement, Sergeant. I don't know whether his sermons deter more people than they attract to the church, but they're always worth hearing. She looked enquiringly at the Yard men.

"I don't know if you are familiar with the excellent works of E F Benson, gentlemen, but the limited social circle in this village mirrors that of Tilling."

Bryce laughed. "I'm very familiar with them – and I won't be so ungallant as to ask whether you yourself have a parallel character from the books."

Mrs Fielding pulled a face. "I think I don't," she said, "although this topic has been discussed in the village. Someone once marked me down as Lucia, which I suppose was intended to be flattering. However, Cameron, my second husband, was alive then, and as the corollary to my being Lucia was that he was cast as Georgie, he wasn't altogether pleased!

"As far as Cunningham's question about whether I knew of anyone with reason to kill George, the answer was a resounding 'no'. I shouldn't have believed he had an enemy in the world – if someone hadn't killed him. I suppose there's no chance this was mistaken identity, Chief Inspector?"

"No chance at all, Mrs Fielding. There's no reason to doubt that Mr Wilcox was the primary target. Nor is there any doubt that Cunningham was set up to be in the right place and the right time to be shot.

"What about Cunningham's question regarding what sort of man Wilcox was?"

"Well, he was very intelligent and erudite, and he could be charming. He could also be very generous. I believe he gave Gregory Mickleburgh useful, but informal and free-of-charge legal advice from time to time – chancel repair liabilities; that sort of thing. He did the same for one or two others, too. I'm not sure what else I said to the reporter."

"After Mr Cunningham had spoken to you, who did you talk to about your conversation with him?" asked Haig.

Mrs Fielding reflected.

"Immediately afterwards, nobody. I returned home, and I think I said something to one of my maids about an impertinent journalist trying to dig up dirt on poor Mr Wilcox. Over the last few days, inevitably, it's cropped up in conversation with several people, although I don't remember any specifics."

"Would I be right in assuming that you haven't been chatting about all this in the Royal Oak, madam?" asked Haig.

Mrs Fielding looked horrified.

"I have not!" she snorted. "Both my husbands used to go in for an occasional drink, but the only time I ever cross the threshold is on flag days, when I go in to shake a tin for the British Legion."

After a short pause, Bryce, in a slightly altered tone of voice, said, "I don't think you've been entirely honest with us, Mrs Fielding. To use a timeworn expression, 'from information received', it would seem that you have more interesting and indeed negative views of the late Mr Wilcox."

There was a lengthy pause. Mrs Fielding sat looking down at her hands. At last she sighed, and looked up again.

"I wonder who the source of your information might be. Only three people in the village and two outside it know any of the facts about what I'm going to tell you – although I suppose one of those may have told others. And there will be a few more – my staff, perhaps, who may have guessed parts of the story.

"A few months after Cameron and Hermione both died, George Wilcox and I started to spend more time together. It was only natural that we should seek each other out, given our shared experience of loss. We'd always got on well – although, as you may have heard, he could be a bit sharp on occasion."

She smiled faintly. "If you cut George as your bridge partner, you made especially sure that you didn't commit some *faux pas* like a revoke. His put-downs could be jolly hurtful, although things always reverted to normal later."

She sighed heavily again. "But in this period, when I wasn't quite myself and was somewhat vulnerable, George began to 'press his suit' as the saying goes. I can't pretend that I was averse to his attentions, although I was still technically in mourning.

"Anyway, he was very persuasive, and rather pushed me into agreeing to marry him before I was properly ready. When I had agreed, he more-or-less took over my affairs, and started dealing with my household and business matters. Probate for my husband's will was not yet granted, and although I was the appointed executor, George took all of that on too. In fairness, I didn't object – everything was still far too much for me, and as a probate specialist he knew the ropes.

"At this point, remember, we had made no public announcement of what I suppose amounted to our engagement – I thought it was indecently early, and he didn't argue the point.

"However, there came a time, perhaps two months after our agreement, when I discovered that he had been buying and selling shares in my name. He didn't have power of attorney, but it seemed he was telephoning orders to the broker that Cameron and I had used, having somehow persuaded the man that he did have the necessary authority. On the same day that I discovered these actions, he dismissed one of my servants without consulting me.

"I confronted him about both matters, and he was entirely unapologetic. 'Far better for a man to deal with these things, my dear', he said.

"I couldn't deny that it was nice to be relieved of some of the business matters. However, I called the broker myself, and discovered the full extent of the transactions supposedly made in my name. I found that George had made several very unwise moves, in both buying and selling. My bank manager did some calculations for me, and it seems George had lost me at least four thousand pounds in less than three months.

"I was very, very, upset. I tackled him about what was really gambling with my money, and told him that what particularly galled me was that he had plenty of money of his own to fritter away. The upshot was that he wouldn't apologise, nor even acknowledge he'd done anything wrong. I told him I'd never marry him, and I never spoke to him again. Incidentally, I reinstated the maid he had sacked."

Mrs Fielding looked downcast and at a loss as she added, "I still can't fathom what caused

George to behave as he did. It was so out of character."

"I suppose you didn't want to make a public thing about it all," said Bryce, "but you could have involved the police."

"My bank manager wanted me to do just that, but, as you say, I didn't want any more people to know." She sighed again.

"There's a particularly sharp humiliation which accompanies betrayal by someone you thought you could trust. Perhaps an older women feels the sense of having embarrassed herself, emotionally as well as financially, more acutely than a younger one might.

"But I'm nothing if not fatalistic, gentlemen. I just licked my wounds, and carried on much as before. George stopped playing bridge and accepting invitations, so it was quite easy to avoid coming into contact with him."

Another silence ensued.

"Well, thank you for telling us all that, Mrs Fielding. I can understand, of course, why you didn't inform Mr Cunningham about your knowledge of Mr Wilcox's character.

"However, we've learned two things today. First, that Mr Wilcox could be blunt and outspoken, although in fairness we've heard that elsewhere. Second, that he wasn't averse to acting dishonestly. Either, or both of those characteristics, could be significant. We have several other people to see, so we'll leave you now.

Thank you for your time."

Mrs Fielding rose with the detectives. Before opening the front door for them she said, "Just one last thing, Chief Inspector. Would I be right in thinking that you misled me just now, and that you didn't actually know any detail about the business with George?"

"Quite right, Mrs Fielding. We were sure there was something, but had no idea what. I'm a bridge player myself, and a finesse was necessary. Like Mr Wilcox, though, I'm not going to apologise. However, I see no reason why this information should ever need to go any further."

"Thank you for that. I hope, by the way, that you don't think that I had anything to do with his murder. I don't shoot – nor would I know where to find somebody else to do the job!"

"I suspect everybody until someone has been convicted in court," replied Bryce, with a smile to reduce the effect of his words.

CHAPTER 9

Outside Mrs Fielding's house, Haig began to laugh. "She fell into that, sir. But I do feel sorry for her. Not pleasant to lose two husbands, and then to be conned out of thousands of pounds while in mourning."

"I'd agree with all of that, Sergeant. However, I'm not sure she told us everything. There may have been something even more embarrassing that she didn't want to mention."

As the detectives walked back towards the centre of the village Bryce was unusually quiet. After a while, and with still a little distance to go before they reached the village shop, Haig decided he should check on his boss. "Are you feeling all right, sir?"

"Oh yes, there's nothing wrong with me. I'm still mulling over whether the lady was still lying to us."

There had been nothing in Mrs Fielding's manner, or answers, which had struck the Sergeant as false in any way. She had responded unhesitatingly – a good indicator of truthfulness, he had often found. He was surprised that his Chief had any reason to even think along those lines, and correspondingly annoyed with himself in case he had missed an important and obvious clue.

"What makes you say that, sir?"

"The paintings. The place they reminded me of wasn't Wales, it was Italy. And I'm pretty sure that's where at least two of them were painted. Either Mrs Fielding's husband lied to her – or she lied to me." Bryce stopped walking and turned to look at his Sergeant. "Given the lady's Mediterranean looks, I can't exclude the possibility that it's the latter. In which case, we must ask ourselves why."

Haig was relieved. He hadn't looked at the paintings at all; and he had never visited either Wales or Italy. He absolved himself of a failure to spot any inconsistency in what Mrs Fielding said, and did his best to come up with an explanation.

"She struck me as honest, sir. Perhaps she genuinely didn't know – just accepted whatever her husband told her?"

Bryce harrumphed.

"Or maybe she does have an Italian connection in her past, but feels it's too soon to say so, if she doesn't have to. You know, in case people still remember where Italy started out in the war and get unpleasant with her about it."

Haig had a further suggestion, but asked himself whether he really wanted to voice it. He decided he did. "Might you be mistaken about the paintings, sir?"

Bryce, pleased that his colleague was confident enough to raise this thought with him, acknowledged that possibility.

"Maybe, Sergeant; maybe. Who's next?"

"Well, as the shop is over there, sir, and Mrs Dodds the shopkeeper and sub-postmistress is on the list, may as well try her and hope that she hears all the gossip."

The two officers stepped into the shop, to the accompaniment of the sound of the brass bell above the door jingling on its spring. In common with similar village stores throughout the country, they had entered the converted front room of a house. A counter, divided into two parts, bisected the room – one, smaller part for the post office, and the other for the shop.

Behind the shop section of the counter were shelves with all manner of provisions, their boxes, bottles, tins and packets organised into attractive displays. Everything from soap to darning wool could often be found in such shops, but there would typically be little – or no – choice of each of the goods on offer. If carbolic soap was stocked, but not preferred for wash day because of its roughness on the hands, villagers would have to make a pilgrimage to a larger village or town to find an alternative.

A short and rotund woman, her greying hair piled up haphazardly on her head, stood behind the counter on the post office side, dealing with an elderly man buying stamps. Both turned as the door opened and took a moment to scrutinise the detectives. Without comment, the pair returned to their transaction – the purchase of two Universal Postal Union commemorative stamps.

With a thruppenny bit and two pennies carefully counted out and passed under the grille, the old boy took his stamps and moved across to the shop counter. In his new position, he asked the same woman for two ounces of Army & Navy sweets, and the same of barley sugars, handing over some more coppers and his ration coupon for the week as he spoke.

Shopkeeper and customer both watched the needle on the scales carefully as the boiled black lozenges rattled out of the glass bottle into the weighing pan, before being poured into a tiny paper bag. The process was repeated for the golden barley twists.

Sergeant Haig was very familiar with this routine. A trip to the local newsagent with Rosie was a happy fortnightly outing for them both. He would lift the child up so that she could hand over her pennies and his coupon (children under five having no ration of their own) and watch her four ounces of dolly mixture weighed and poured into the bag. Haig's wife, Fiona, would dole out the treats to the little girl until the next shop visit, two ounces per week being more than sufficient, she felt, for a young child.

The elderly man dropped the little bags into his greatcoat pockets and touched the peak of his cap to the postmistress. "Thanking you," he said, and left the shop.

"You'll be the police from London, then?" enquired the woman from behind her counter. "I'm Sylvia Dodds, as you will have seen over my door. What can I do for you, gentlemen?"

Bryce gave their names, and asked if it was all right to carry out the interview in the public area of the shop.

"No skin off my nose," she replied. "I've got nothing to hide – go ahead and ask what you like."

"You talked to Mr Cunningham, the *Examiner* reporter, a couple of days ago," said the DCI. "You've probably heard that he's also been shot dead."

"I heard today – poor Mr Allen too. What a wicked world we do live in."

"We have Mr Cunningham's notes that he made regarding all the conversations around the village, but it would be helpful to hear from you directly about what he asked, and what you told him."

It seemed that Mrs Dodds had been asked much the same questions as Mrs Fielding, and her answers to the reporter had apparently been similar.

Bryce gave the post mistress a cynical smile.

"You're in a unique position in this village, Mrs Dodds – don't tell me that there's anything going on here you don't know about." His expression hardened. "It's understandable to try to keep village secrets away from newspaper people, but I warn you not to keep them from us. This is a murder enquiry, remember – three murders, actually.

"So why not tell us what you know about the late Mr Wilcox, that you chose not to tell Mr Cunningham?"

Mrs Dodds leaned over the counter toward the officers to rest on her forearms between bags of flour on one side, and a pile of tins on the other.

In a resigned voice she said, "Yes, you're right, of course. None of us wanted to tell that reporter anything. He had the cottage in the village, but you can't say he lived here, and he wouldn't ever be a villager when he only came for an odd day or two. He'd been coming and going for a few months, I heard, but hadn't been in my shop once, and had never so much as spoken to me 'til he came round with his notebook.

"As for Mr Wilcox, he was always polite to me, and paid his bill on time. I hear things, as you say, and I picked up that Mr Wilcox had a less pleasant side. He did something bad to Mrs Fielding, by all accounts. Stole money, I heard. And he crossed Mrs Redfern too, and that's a stupid thing to do – she's every bit as tough as the old Squire was." She shook her head, causing the loose curls of her upswept hair to shift from side to side.

"But I honestly don't know what that

trouble was. You'd have to speak to her yourselves. And if she won't tell you, maybe you'll find that her maid, Gladys, knows. Beyond that, I really can't tell you any more."

The shop doorbell clanged, and a woman in her thirties entered, carrying a shopping basket. "Good afternoon, Sylvia," she said warmly, and then eyed the policemen.

"I'm guessing you must be more police officers. I saw two others wandering around before, so you're certainly putting some manpower on the case! If you're talking to everyone, by all means deal with me here and now. I'm Lavinia Temple, by the way; my husband is the local medic."

Bryce performed the introductions. It was news to Mrs Temple that Scotland Yard had been called in.

"Would you like to complete your shopping before we talk?"

"No, you're busy people. Let's go outside and get it done now." With a smile for the postmistress she said, "Back in a minute, Sylvia."

Mrs Temple made her way to a bench on the green a few yards away, and sat down, placing her basket beside her.

"There's room for all three of us, but I expect you want to watch my face to see if I'm lying," she announced matter-of-factly.

Both policemen grinned.

"As you say, Mrs Temple. Well, you're

presumably aware that Marcus Cunningham, the journalist who half lived in the village, is dead."

Already sitting upright on the high-backed seat, the doctor's wife momentarily became even more rigid. "I wasn't aware, Chief Inspector!" was her astounded response. "My husband is taking a couple of days off, and neither of us left the house yesterday – nor today until just now. Don't tell me Mr Cunningham was murdered too?"

"Yes. Also Desmond Allen."

"Good God! Just as well I'm sitting down. Would it be in in order to ask if all three are connected? If that were so, I'd have to suppose that poor Cunningham dug a bit too deeply for someone's comfort."

"They are certainly connected, and your supposition may well be correct. We're interviewing everyone he spoke to – and your name is mentioned in his notes. When he talked to you, what did he ask, and what, exactly, did you say?"

"While I recover my breath, I'd just like take issue with your saying he 'half lived in the village'. He did no such thing. I have no idea why a man of his background took the cottage – as I understand it, it isn't fit for human habitation – but he's not spent above a night or two a week here anyway. Nowhere near 'half living'."

Mrs Temple proceeded to give her own recollections of her conversation with the reporter. It was as if she had overheard what

Mesdames Fielding and Dodds had said. Her report was practically identical to theirs in all respects, and added nothing to what the detectives already knew.

"Very well, Mrs Temple. We've spoken to a number of people, and we're hearing things about Mr Wilcox that nobody saw fit to tell a journalist. For good reasons, no doubt. Those reasons, I need hardly emphasise, do not apply when talking to police officers investigating three murders.

"So let's have it, please."

Mrs Temple laughed. "Refreshingly direct, Chief Inspector. Very well. Just remember that this is only hearsay. Gossip, really. I pick it up – one can hardly avoid that in a village – but I'm not in the habit of repeating it to anyone other than my husband. If this wasn't so important, I shouldn't repeat it to you.

"George could be a tad nasty. He annoyed the Vicar; he seriously upset Mrs Redfern at the hall, and also Christina Fielding. And there's a rumour that he fell out with a major landowner, Vincent Eddington.

"I'm only privy to one of those matters, and that's Christina's, but you must speak to her for details."

"That's all right, Mrs Temple; we've heard something of all four, and Mrs Fielding has already put us in the picture. We've also talked to the Vicar, and Inspector Catchpole is interviewing Mr Eddington as we speak. We hope to see Mrs

Redfern shortly.

"Is there anything else you feel you can tell us, that we should know?"

The doctor's wife shook her head slowly. "I'm still in shock. No, I can't think of anything. But what about Desmond Allen? Nobody called Archie to say they'd found his body. Nor for Cunningham, either."

"Not a deliberate attempt to exclude your husband, Mrs Temple. Mr Allen was found by the police during a search for his body, when we guessed he was already dead. The police surgeon was called to the site.

"As for Cunningham, he was killed in Liverpool Street station, and until his death was connected to Ashton, the City of London police were dealing with it."

Mrs Temple shook her head in bewilderment.

"I realise you can't give me details, but could you just say if what seems to be obvious is true – that these men were killed by some sort of paid killer?"

"I think we can safely say that in two of the cases, yes. We don't think there was a contract out on Mr Allen – it was probably just his misfortune to be where he was that day."

"So should we all be worried in case we're next?"

"Not at all. Immediately after killing Cunningham, the gunman was himself shot dead by a passing soldier."

"Good for him!" exclaimed Mrs Temple with feeling. "I'd better go and do my bit of shopping," she said, standing up and picking up her basket. "You presumably know where I live if you have any more questions. Good luck with Cynthia Redfern."

"Her husband wasn't on Cunningham's list, was he?" asked Bryce when the doctor's wife had gone.

"No, sir.

"Hmm. Curious. I should have thought that the Vicar and the Doctor would be the two villagers who – after the sub-postmistress – would be likely to have the most information."

"Perhaps Cunningham had already come across one or more of the bits of gossip that we've been hearing, and so didn't need to see anyone else," suggested Haig.

"Yes, that's likely. But all the people we've seen are adamant that they didn't tell him anything useful. I'm beginning to wonder if he picked up some gossip *before* Wilcox was killed – old Spraggons said Cunningham drank in the Royal Oak from time to time, so he could have heard something there."

"You mean that when Wilcox was killed, he realised that he might already have some information about motive, and started to ask around? Dangerous thing to do, that."

"Very. Let's go back to the car and then find the hall."

***

They found the entrance gates easily enough, and Haig drove for several hundred yards along a drive – unmade, albeit in very good repair. The hall turned out to be a more modest affair than either had subconsciously expected – a two storey Georgian cuboid of no particular architectural merit, Bryce thought.

Haig pulled up quite near the front door, alongside another car – a Hooper drophead Bentley, probably from 1937, finished in sky blue. Bryce, who owned a Triumph Roadster himself, knew that his car was as nothing compared to this beauty. To the side of the house they could see a man cleaning another vehicle, only slightly older than the Bentley and one which had also been an expensive model in its day – a Daimler Light Fifteen, in black and cream. Beside the Daimler was a third vehicle, an Austin Seven 'Ruby', the oldest of the trio by a couple of years, and at the opposite end of the scale in price and status.

Reluctantly tearing his eyes away from the Bentley, Bryce rang the doorbell. The door opened to reveal a short man, dressed in a butler's day clothes.

Bryce explained who they were and what they were investigating, and asked to see Mrs Redfern. He handed the man one of his 'reserve' cards, rather than the simple one he habitually offered. The Butler glanced at it, hesitated for a moment, and then, perhaps impressed by the 'MC, MA (Cantab)' after Bryce's rank and name, and 'Barrister-at-Law' underneath, stepped aside to admit them. They were showed into a grandly furnished withdrawing room. Assuring the detectives that he would see if his mistress was free, the Butler backed out of the room and pulled the double doors shut.

Presently, the door opened again, and a slim grey-haired lady entered. Beautifully dressed, and with the deportment of a former ballerina, she could have been any age between fifty and seventy. As she drew closer, Bryce decided that his upper estimate was the more accurate.

Clutching Bryce's card, she greeted the detectives. "Good afternoon gentlemen. You'll be here regarding the death of George Wilcox, no doubt." She shook both men firmly by the hand – not the usual lightweight handshake many females used, the DCI noted.

"Do sit down. Can I offer you some refreshment?"

This was declined with thanks.

"If you change your minds, do say. Now, I've been expecting you. Or, more accurately, I've been expecting a visit from the Suffolk police. I had not realised that Scotland Yard had been called in. It seems a little premature – the man's only been dead a few days. Is the case really beyond the powers of the local people?"

Bryce explained the reason for the Yard's

involvement. Like Lavinia Temple, Mrs Redfern hadn't heard about the deaths of Allen and Cunningham.

"I see," she said, sharing Mr Spraggons' placid response in being neither surprised nor upset. "Whatever are we all coming to? Three murders in or relating to my beloved village? Astonishing! I was born twenty years before Queen Victoria died, and it is an undoubted fact that there have been some horrendous events during my time on this earth. These outrages obviously don't rank even close to the worst of those – but it is the first time that such things have come so near to home, as it were.

"I'd heard that there was a reporter in the village asking questions, but I never met him. What is it you think I can help you with, Chief Inspector?"

"You said you were expecting a visit, ma'am, and we in our turn have heard that you may have had reason to dislike Mr Wilcox. Perhaps you could tell us about that?"

Mrs Redfern smiled. "Oh yes. You see, I'd known George for many years. My late husband used that firm for almost all his legal business – as indeed his father and grandfather had before him. Another partner handled much of the work – land law and conveyancing and so on. A third partner dealt with the rare occasions where some sort of court work was required. George only handled our wills and trusts.

"Because he lived in the village, we saw far more of him than we did the partners who did the bulk of our work. He and his late wife Hermione played a good hand of bridge, which our limited social circle here enjoys."

She paused, and Bryce filled the gap.

"We do hear that he was a bit of a stickler when playing – woe betide a partner who committed a *faux pas* like a revoke, for example."

Mrs Redfern roared with laughter.

"A bit of a stickler! Diplomatically, but not very accurately put, Chief Inspector. George had a caustic tongue and could be appallingly rude – I've been on the receiving end, myself. But his temper only ever lasted a matter of seconds, and for some reason nobody ever bore him a grudge over something that was, I believe, largely outside his control; a constitutional flaw, if you will. For most of each game he was emollient, and an excellent companion.

"No, it wasn't his flashes of temper which caused the falling out between us. It was a series of examples of bad legal advice – arguably criminally bad – which he delivered over a very short period.

"People die, gentlemen, but in our village there are several who each lost their spouse almost simultaneously. In particular Christina Fielding, me, and George himself. When that happens, perhaps it can be said as a generalisation that the balance of the survivor's mind is disturbed, at least temporarily. I believe that may have happened, quite seriously, in George's case – and in mine too, in a different way.

"I was not yet ready to take on the many burdens which Lawrence had shouldered so well, and I allowed George to act for me in my business affairs. I should explain that we don't employ an agent. My son is in the Royal Air Force serving overseas, and it will be a year or more before he is ready to take over the management of the estate.

"Anyway, George instigated several actions, and from time-to-time placed documents in front of me for signature. I noticed that one was a land transfer, but when I questioned it he just said something about it making sense to rationalise my land holdings. Frankly, I was stupidly naïve, but I had no reason to distrust the man.

"After a few months, I felt more able to act for myself – to become the 'squire', so to speak. But looking into what had been happening, I was disconcerted – horrified actually – to find that he had disposed of several hundred acres of prime farmland, for prices which were well beneath even the current low market value. He had also given Ezra Wellbeloved, one of our tenant farmers, notice to quit. I'm ashamed to say that on more than one occasion I had not read the papers put in front of me.

"When I took these things up with George, he said that farmer wasn't working the land to its best advantage – how he suddenly became an expert in land husbandry I really don't know.

As for the low sale prices, he used historic fluctuations as a fig leaf for his poor judgement.

"By this time I was pretty well back to my normal state, and I gave him a real dressing down. I pointed out that it was absurd to sell good arable acreage at distressed seller prices when I had no need to realise any assets."

Haig looked up from his notetaking. "How did Mr Wilcox take his telling off, ma'am?"

"He got very angry, and in the end I banished him from my house. There was nothing I could do about the sale of the land, but I rescinded the notice to quit, and apologised to Wellbeloved for what I euphemistically said was a misunderstanding.

"I haven't yet spoken to George's old firm, although I shall be doing so – I have an appointment to see Duncan Congreve, the senior partner, next week. I was going to take his advice about reporting George to the Law Society, but that would be pointless now.

"You should also speak to Christina if you haven't already done so; she also suffered considerably because of George's actions – actions which I am sure in earlier days he would never have countenanced."

Mrs Redfern smiled when she had finished.

"The expressions on your faces, gentlemen – I wish I had a camera to hand!"

Bryce smiled too.

"The Sergeant and I are probably both

thinking the same thing, Mrs Redfern. More than once in recent cases, we found on investigation that the victim was not quite as pure and innocent as was thought at first."

"No doubt you have me high up on your list of suspects, Chief Inspector. Until you arrived, I assumed someone had simply shot George, and it is a fact that I possess several guns and do a lot of shooting – rather well, as it happens. I did also worry that Wellbeloved might have done it – I don't think for one minute that he swallowed my story about a 'misunderstanding'. However, now that you say the reporter was shot in London, I assume you are looking for a professional killer. Let me just say that I really have not the faintest clue as to how to find such a person, and I doubt if Wellbeloved could either – and that's before considerations of cost. I know the old saw tells us that 'life is cheap', but I really can't believe that's the case for a paid killer. Anyway, I'd rescinded his notice to quit very quickly, several days before George was killed."

"Actually, ma'am, we aren't looking for the gunman," said Haig. "The man who shot the journalist was himself shot by an armed soldier seconds later."

"Oh, excellent," said Mrs Redfern, "I hope the man is given a medal."

"It may be excellent in one way," replied the DCI, but unfortunately it means we can't question the gunman about who commissioned the killings. The police are searching his property this afternoon, but I'll be very surprised if he kept any records."

Following a sign from Bryce, both officers stood up.

"Thank you very much for your candour, Mrs Redfern. We will get to the bottom of this."

The Lady of the Manor saw them to the front door herself, although the butler was hovering in the hall.

"Shall we see the farmer, sir?" asked Haig, as he steered the Wolseley back down the drive.

Bryce considered the question. "It may come to that, but not just yet, I think. Actually, there are other possibilities. I should have asked if her staff were aware of the happenings. Butlers can be fanatically loyal," he added cryptically.

"Let's get back to Woodbridge, and see if there's any news from 'The Smoke'."

CHAPTER 10

While the Yard officers were speaking to Mrs Redfern, the Suffolk policemen arrived at Mr Eddington's residence near Woolpit. It was not a particularly large house, being similar in size to that of Mrs Fielding, but it was clear to see that no expense was spared in its upkeep. Sergeant Jephson pulled the bell handle, and the resulting jangle could be heard outside. The owner of the house came to the door himself. On learning who the visitors were. he invited them inside, and took them into a pleasant book-lined study.

"Sit down, gentlemen. I imagine you're looking into the death of George Wilcox. How can I help?"

"We understand that you had granted him shooting rights over land in his village, sir," said Catchpole.

"Quite correct. And, as you may have heard elsewhere, we had a falling out recently. I'll give you the history. Hearing it, you'll probably put me near the top of your list of suspects, but I'm not guilty.

"I have a superb shoot on the estate here, gentlemen, and for years had no interest in making any similar use of my land in and around Ashton. Ten or twelve years ago, Wilcox and another chap, Desmond Allen, wanted to acquire some rights for rough shooting. They approached me with a proposition. As a result I agreed to allow them to shoot over about two hundred and fifty acres of deciduous woodland, pasture, and some arable land. The fee was set at one hundred guineas a year, each man paying half. Wilcox drew up a formal agreement, and the three of us signed it before a witness.

"A few months ago, my son was looking into ways of improving the return on our land holdings, and suggested creating a pheasant shoot in Ashton – building a hatchery, and so on. I dug out the contract with Allen and Wilcox. To be perfectly honest, I'd never read it properly all those years before. When Max read it, he was horrified.

"Wilcox was a solicitor, of course, and he'd drafted the agreement in such a way – and so tightly – that I could never grant anyone else permission to shoot over that land. I couldn't even do so myself, actually!

"Max took it to our own legal advisor, who hadn't been involved in the original arrangement."

Seeing Catchpole's eyebrows lifting into his hairline at this, Eddington gave a self-deprecating explanation. "Yes, it was absurdly penny-pinching of me not to get a lawyer to look over it for me before I signed. But I won't be the first – or the last – prosperous person to watch the pennies. Making money is the way to get rich, gentlemen; not spending more than necessary is the way to keep it.

"Anyway, my man thought the contract was watertight, but sought the advice of a barrister, who concurred. The lawyers made two suggestions. One was that we could offer to buy out the two rights holders, but with the expectation that it wouldn't be cheap. The other was that we could offer Wilcox and Allen the right to participate in some or all future shoots in return for ceding the rights.

"A couple of weeks ago, Max visited Wilcox to discuss matters. He was given short shrift – sent away with a flea in his ear.

"Apparently Wilcox said: 'Your father entered into a valid legal contract, properly witnessed. If he didn't read it properly before he signed, that's his problem. It's been in operation now for over twelve years without a hiccup, and your father has been happily pocketing the agreed fees throughout that time – so the courts certainly won't set it aside. And as neither of your offers is acceptable, I'm not going to agree to alter it either. The contract ends only when both Allen and I are dead.'"

Catchpole shifted in his seat. "You are indeed racing to the top of the list, sir. Are you aware that Mr Allen has also been murdered?"

Eddington stared at him. "No, I wasn't. But neither death is anything to do with me. No matter how it might look now it seems the contract is at an end after all, he added."

"There's been a third associated murder, sir – a local reporter named Cunningham. All three carried out with a sawn-off shotgun."

"I see. Sounds like a professional hitman. Not my style, paying someone to do my dirty work. Never heard of this reporter."

"No? Well, he was one of your tenants in Ashton – another link with you."

For the first time, Eddington looked surprised. "I have a good number of properties across the area, Inspector. They're all handled by my land agent, and I have nothing to do with them. I must say I thought they were all occupied by people who work either for me or for one of my tenant farmers. I assume a cottage became vacant and Parkinson didn't have an employee wanting to take it.

"I can see you are just itching to arrest me, but I assure you that would be a serious mistake. I shot a few people in the Great War, but nobody since. You'll have to look for someone else with a motive, Inspector; you're wasting time here."

"I'm not arresting you now, sir," Catchpole told him. "I'm not in charge of this investigation. I'll report to the Scotland Yard Chief Inspector and see what he says. We'll be in touch, without doubt."

"In that case, you can go," said Eddington,

standing up, "I have work to do."

CHAPTER 11

Bryce and Haig, arriving back at Woodbridge, found the Desk Sergeant had little information to report. DI Catchpole had called to say that he would be back after six o'clock; there were no messages from London.

Bryce consulted his watch. "I feel like a walk while there's some daylight left," he said. "There's an old curiosity here on the river – a tide mill. I'd like to see it, although it probably isn't a very beautiful building."

The local officer pointed them in the right direction, and the two Yard men set off. On arrival at the River Deben, the mill stood out; being some three storeys high it towered over everything else. As the DCI had anticipated, it looked rather decrepit. Still in commercial operation, its white timber cladding looked in need of repair and paint.

Haig looked at the building doubtfully.

"I've heard of tide mills, guv, but never seen one as far as I know. How on earth does it work?"

"Twice a day, the incoming tide fills a reservoir – that water over there." Bryce pointed.

"About seven acres, I think, and six feet or so deep. That's a huge weight of water. At high tide, the sluice gate is closed, and the stored water is gradually released to turn a water wheel.

"There are only two of these left in England now, I believe, although at one time they were quite common – not nearly as common as windmills and river-fed water mills, of course. Very few in Scotland, though.

"Apparently there was a tide mill here for over seven hundred years – not this present structure, obviously."

Sergeant Haig was impressed by the simplicity of the principle. "Our forefathers were pretty good at finding free power to harness, then. I can see the potential from wind and rivers, but I'd never have thought of capturing the tide!"

"It's believed the technology goes back to the Romans. But the river estuary had to be just right – far enough from the sea to avoid any risk of being overwhelmed, but at a point which is still tidal."

Bryce pointed to the other side of the water. "Just across the river, Alex, up that hill, is the Sutton Hoo ship burial site, where the wonderful treasure was found, just at the outbreak of the war."

"Aye, I've seen some of that in the British Museum, guv. But they don't seem to be sure who was buried with it."

"No. Likely to be a king of the East Angles, though. I believe Raedwald is favourite. In this area, I suppose not much written history has survived thirteen or so centuries."

Haig grinned. "When you look at church gravestones dating back even a couple of hundred years, many of them are illegible. So even if the Angles had stuck a sign up, not much chance of reading it today!"

"Very true," laughed the DCI. "We'd better get back."

Catchpole and Jephson still hadn't arrived, and the London men went along to the little incident room. They had hardly sat down before the DI joined them.

"What have you done with Jephson?" enquired Bryce.

"Dropped him off at his house in Ipswich," replied Catchpole. He's had a couple of late nights, so I thought I'd get him home more or less on time for once!"

"Fair enough," said the DCI, "but a shame that he'll miss another meal! I hope you'll join us again, Catchpole, although we'll understand if you want to get back."

"I'd like to stay if you're kind enough to invite me, sir. My landlady is very understanding – and more often than not I do manage to get in for my meals at a reasonable time. But since I last saw you I've become attached to a young lady. If, as I hope, we eventually marry, Alicia will also need to accept a detective's erratic hours!"

Bryce grinned. "Congratulations. May you be

as happy in your marriage as we both are. And since it's your constabulary that picks up the tab, in effect you're the host here, so my inviting you to a meal is really a bit cheeky!"

His colleagues laughed.

"Let's spend half an hour or so exchanging information, and then take ourselves to the Bull.

"You kick off for us, please Sergeant."

Haig had expected this task would be delegated to him, and was ready. He briskly and accurately outlined what they had learned from each of the four women they had interviewed.

Catchpole remarked that there seemed to be some possibilities for new suspects.

"Yes," said Bryce. "But let's hear what you've found, and then we can review the situation."

"Taking our three interviewees in reverse order," began the DI, "Mrs Cunningham was hopeless. Nice enough woman, although obviously still upset. She took us into her son's room. He had a desk in there, but the only papers were things like car insurance and registration documents. Nothing work-related at all.

"She doesn't really know why he took the hovel, as she calls his cottage. I still wonder if there's some connection with his taking the lease and the subsequent events, but I'm blowed if I can see what.

"Mytton was a washout. He told us that he behaved irrationally and badly over the will, and that a couple of years ago he contacted his stepsister to apologise. She accepted the apology, and they're now on good terms. So much so that when he married and had a baby, Miss Orbell became godmother. I'll contact her to check, but I must say Mytton seemed completely truthful.

"He also had the grace to say that he was ashamed of his shouting at his barrister and the solicitor. He didn't know about Wilcox's death.

"Last but not least, Vincent Eddington. He'll certainly have to go onto the list of suspects." Catchpole described the interview.

"He was quite blasé about the whole thing, sir. Fact is, though, he's certainly rich enough to easily afford Dean's price. And the son is an unknown quantity – we didn't see him. Maybe his 'style' isn't the same as the father's."

"All very interesting, Inspector. But there's another aspect that you haven't mentioned. We've assumed that Allen only died because he saw the gunman. But if the Eddingtons are the initiators, they would need to remove both men to recover the rights. One wouldn't do. What if the contract wasn't just for Wilcox, but for Allen too?"

Catchpole and Haig looked more cheerful.

"That's a good point, sir," exclaimed Haig. "We should maybe look into young Eddington?"

Catchpole nodded vigorously. "I shouldn't have missed that point, sir, but it would certainly be a logical solution to all this."

"Perhaps. We must certainly interview Max Eddington. However, ask yourselves this. The

Eddingtons live, what, twenty miles away? If one of them is responsible, how did he know about Cunningham?

"And nothing we've heard in Ashton suggests Cunningham knew anything of the Eddingtons. Cunningham didn't mention either father or son in his notebook, and as far as we know had never spoken to them – I accept that the cottage tenancy would have been arranged through the agent. In fact, if the Vicar hadn't pointed us towards Vincent Eddington, we might never have drawn him into our enquiry.

"So although the business of the shooting rights looks exceedingly suspicious, I'm not convinced."

Bryce's subordinates mentally accepted – with reluctance – that what the DCI said was also logical, and their momentary excitement died away.

"Before going to eat, let's briefly review the motives and possible suspects we have found so far.

"First the information from the Vicar. Unpleasant behaviour in committee or when playing cards can hardly be considered motive for murder – not by a sane person, anyway. And it seems that Wilcox resigned from the PCC, and also stopped playing bridge, months ago. Can we assume that his withdrawal from social life was precipitated by his spats with the two ladies? Or could there be yet another reason that we haven't yet realised?"

"I think his withdrawal must be because of the incidents with the ladies, sir," said Catchpole. "But I think there must be something different which triggered his murder. It seems clear he had some sort of brainstorm to start acting out of character, and probably seriously upset someone else."

"I think the brainstorm was always going to come in the end," remarked Haig. "Someone who has those sudden outbursts doesn't look very stable to me. But I agree with Mr Catchpole – Wilcox went too far with someone. Either that or it was the Eddingtons."

Bryce nodded. "All right. Now, the Vicar seemed quite keen to draw our attention towards other people. Views on him?"

"I suppose it's possible that he was the one who had some more serious bone of contention with Wilcox which we haven't yet discovered," suggested the DI.

"Yes – we may need to put a few more questions to him. And ask a few other villagers about him."

"Not all vicars are poor, sir," put in Haig, "we could make enquiries to see if he has any private means."

"Also a valid suggestion, Sergeant. Then we have Mrs Fielding. A very strong motive. Wilcox fiddled her out of a large sum of money, and it could also be the case that he trifled with her affections. She talked to Cunningham too. I got the impression she's a very strong-willed woman. Yes, she wasn't herself when she lost her second husband, but when she recovered she fairly sent Wilcox packing. And she also had the funds to pay for the job. Comments?"

"True, sir, but how would a middle-aged widow, living what seems to be a sheltered life in the wilds of Suffolk, know how to approach a contract killer?"

"I can't argue with that point, Sergeant," said the DI with a self-deprecating smile.

"Next comes the Lady of the Manor. Again, a first-class motive. And again, she seems to have at least as much get-up-and-go as Mrs Fielding – another formidable woman. And certainly ample funds to pay Dean. But your point about a countrywoman finding a contract killer is valid here as well, Sergeant. Anyone voting for her?"

Both officers shook their heads slowly, although Catchpole added that he certainly wouldn't take her off the list.

"Associated with her we have the farmer, Wellbeloved. And, I suppose, any member of her staff who equated Mrs Redfern to Henry the Second, and perhaps took some rhetorical remark about 'who will rid me of this turbulent solicitor?' too seriously.

"I agree that any of those are probably more likely than Mrs Redfern herself, sir," said Haig. "But we come back again to the question of funding."

"Yes, but what if Mrs Redfern wasn't quite as innocent as Henry is supposed to have been, and actually asked one of her men to sort things out – and agreed to pay for the work?" said Catchpole.

"That does seem a possibility," agreed the DCI, "although we're back to the unlikely thought of an untravelled countryman searching in London for a suitable professional assassin.

"Also, a bit of a job to prove it. We don't have grounds to ask for a court order to look at her bank accounts. Worth bearing in mind, though.

"Finally, we have one or both Eddingtons. We needn't talk about them any more now, but clearly they rank high on the list, as you said, Inspector.

"Can either of you think of any other possible candidate? We must remain on the lookout for someone whom we haven't yet heard about, of course."

The DI and DS shook their heads, but Catchpole voiced an opinion.

"We all seem to be agreed that the killer must have been commissioned – or at least the order must have been issued – by someone with money. Also, there must be a connection with the village, because of Cunningham's questions. It's clear that the village is divided into two – those who are invited to play bridge, and those who aren't. Seems to me that we don't need to look very hard outside the bridge-playing clique – plus the Eddingtons, who probably play bridge in their own circle!"

The other two officers smiled.

"It is an interesting divide, certainly," said Bryce. "Like Tilling, as Mrs Fielding said. However, just as in Benson's fiction, not all the bridge players have money. Some – perhaps the Vicar and his wife – have comparatively little. Others, like Doctor and Mrs Temple, probably have a little more, but nothing like the deep pockets of a Redfern or a Fielding. I doubt if a country GP could afford two of Dean's fees."

"I see that, sir," replied Haig, "but I'm still with Mr Catchpole in that the person who started all this is almost certainly in the card group."

"Oh, I don't really disagree. We do need to trawl the rest of the village to see if anyone else is in the bridge set – or, equally importantly, has money. I think by now we should probably have heard of anyone else with a grudge, but we must check.

"However, I've been thinking of another possibility. I think this is extremely unlikely, but just suppose Dean was paid by results, after the job was done, rather than in advance. Anyone, whether moneyed or not, could issue the instructions."

His colleagues both looked unenthusiastic at this idea.

"Sorry, sir, I can't buy that one," said Haig. "Anyone who ordered a murder to be carried out by a professional killer, all the time knowing that he couldn't meet the bill, would be mad. He'd know that he'd soon be a target himself."

"Agreed, sir," added the DI. "I've never met a professional hitman, admittedly, but I can't believe people like that don't want the full fee up front."

Bryce grinned. "I'm not arguing the point, because I'm sure you're both right, but until we have a credible suspect we can't eliminate anyone at this stage.

"Just one last thought. What is the significance in Cunningham's move to Ashton?"

"It's certainly very odd, sir," replied Catchpole. "His mother's house in Ipswich must have been very comfortable for him. And even though Mrs Cunningham was upset, she seemed a nice old soul. Yet he chose to rent and occasionally occupy a hovel which really isn't in much better condition than an outbuilding for livestock.

"But I can't for the life of me see any connection with Wilcox."

"Nor can I," said the DCI. "He came to Ashton some time before Wilcox was killed. It's still niggling me that the Ashton entries in Cunningham's current notebook are so useless." He shook his head. "Perhaps Dearden was right – if Cunningham thought he was onto something big he might go to unusual lengths to ensure that nobody else caught a whiff of his story.

"We never actually saw the old notebooks Dearden mentioned. Remiss of me, although I can't think there's anything useful in them. Inspector, get hold of Jephson, and tell him to go to the newspaper office again in the morning. He can remove all the old notebooks and meet us in Ashton later.

"I'm surprised we still haven't heard anything about the search of Dean's property, but nothing we can do about that. In the morning we'll decide what's next on the to-do list. When you've spoken to Jephson, let's go and eat."

***

The food at the Bull had been well-received by the officers the previous evening, and as they sat in the bar all three looked forward to another satisfying meal.

"I suppose in one way your set-up in Suffolk is similar to ours in London, Trevor," remarked Bryce. "East Suffolk has Ipswich with its own constabulary sitting in the middle, just like we have the City police in the middle of the Met."

"That's right," replied Catchpole. "It isn't ideal. I reckon we'll merge within my lifetime, but for the moment there are lots of vested interests against the idea."

"I wouldn't bet on the Met merging with the City police in my lifetime," smiled Bryce. "The City may be tiny, both in terms of area and resident population, but its influence is immense in many ways.

"A few weeks ago I asked my team where

they saw themselves in ten years. Alex here hoped to be an inspector by then – and I told him I expect him to reach it inside two. What about you, Trevor?"

"I was very lucky to be made a DI as young as I was, guv. So if I stay in Suffolk I can't look for any promotion for a very long time. However, if I manage to keep my copybook blot free, I suppose I might look to make DCI towards the end of your ten-year timescale. After that, I'll have maybe twenty years in which to make superintendent before I retire."

"I'm not so sure," mused Bryce. "I foresee considerable expansion of most police forces over the next few years. I also think that some of those presently holding senior positions will start to be eased out, and with good reason. Certainly a few in the Met are like some of the First War generals – devoid of initiative and stuck in the past. If I'm right, it won't necessarily be a question of waiting until someone retires or dies in harness.

"So I suggest your chances are actually pretty good, Trevor`. I'm forever saying I'm not a betting man. But if I were, I'd put a few bob on your reaching superintendent by forty-five."

Catchpole's expression as he looked at his temporary chief was much the same as Haig's when told about the two-year forecast for his own promotion a few weeks before. He shook his head in semi-disbelief.

Haig wondered if the informal situation

would allow him to ask about how the boss saw his own future. It was generally reckoned that Bryce would at least reach assistant commissioner, but Haig thought that the DCI was so modest he'd probably say he might reach superintendent in fifteen years. Before he could decide whether he dared ask, Catchpole changed the subject, and the moment was lost.

"Do you still have your lovely Triumph Roadster, guv?"

"I do, yes. And it is indeed lovely. There are times, though, when I see another car and realise there are even nicer ones around! Today it was a drophead Bentley at Ashton Manor. Nearly ten years older than mine, but undeniably more desirable. I hate to think what Veronica would say if I brought one home – although as you'll remember, Alex, she sometimes used to drive a big Bentley belonging to the Sherwoods."

Haig nodded, with a grin – he knew how much that case had altered his chief's life.

"Sherwood – was that the case down in Hampshire?" asked Catchpole?

Bryce nodded. "Yes – all solved, but not an entirely satisfactory outcome in one or two respects. Come to think of it, Alex and I have had a couple of cases like that recently. Let's hope this one leaves us feeling completely content."

A waitress invited them to move into the dining room, where they discussed various topics over another decent meal, accompanied this time by a surprisingly good bottle of burgundy.

Haig, whose confidence had soared in the time he'd been working with the DCI, even felt able to rib the Suffolk inspector.

"Not sure if you realise this, Trevor, but you may not be qualified to work with the guv full-time."

Recognising that the junior man wasn't being rude, Catchpole played along. "Why's that, Alex?"

"Because he has certain crucial requirements. Before you can even get in his car you have to be a non-smoker. You need a deep knowledge of railways and locomotives, and a keen interest in cricket. You need to know when to remain silent, and when to speak. When he's your passenger, you mustn't drive too slowly, or too fast."

Bryce roared with laughter, to Haig's pleasure.

Catchpole grinned too. "I don't think I'd score too badly," he replied. "We don't have a lot of railways around here, and only a couple of named trains. But I could talk about the Southwold Railway, closed since 1929. Or the Mid-Suffolk Light Railway, which was already in receivership at the time of the Grouping, but was somehow absorbed into the LNER, and struggled along for the next twenty-five years. That'll almost certainly be closed in the next year or so.

"I admit I'm not so good on cricket.

Although I follow England of course, Suffolk is only a minor county, so there are no first-class teams to see.

"As for smoking, as it happens I'm one of the twenty percent of adults who don't – but I'd just point out that I was a passenger in the Triumph not long ago, and I wasn't asked to prove my non-smoking pedigree!"

"An oversight, Trevor," said Bryce, still laughing. "But if you'd tried to light up on that journey, you'd have been deposited at the roadside in a matter of seconds.

"Mind you, squashed in as you were between Vee and me, I doubt if you could have reached into your pocket to bring out a packet of cigarettes anyway!

"All in all though, I think you've done enough to become an honorary member."

Not for the first time, Haig was thankful that chance had brought him to his present post, and allowed him to work with the first senior officer he'd encountered whom he could respect both professionally as well as personally.

CHAPTER 12

In the police station the following morning, the Desk Sergeant reported that DC Barker had asked the DCI to call. He also handed over an envelope, which he said Dr Quilter had delivered personally not half an hour before. Bryce was impressed – he'd liked the Police Surgeon during their previous dealings, but to drive out to Woodbridge after being up late doing the *post mortem* really did display dedication to duty.

Reaching the incident room, he tore open the envelope and quickly read the contents. There was nothing unexpected. Allen's cause of death was just the same as Wilcox's and Cunningham's – a shotgun blast to the torso. The only difference was that only three pellets had struck Allen – but two of those had penetrated his lungs, and the other his heart. Quilter refrained from estimating the distance from which the shot had been fired, simply saying it must have been rather greater than that which had killed Wilcox. He pointed out that, if the shotgun had been double-barrelled, given the spread of shot he couldn't say whether one or both barrels had been fired.

Bryce pushed the report over to Haig, and picked up the telephone. After the usual connection difficulties, Barker eventually came on the line. Even with the receiver pressed to the DCI's ear, Haig could hear the excitement in the young Constable's voice. However, in reality he had little to report.

Barker spoke for some time, with Bryce asking the odd question in between. Eventually he replaced the receiver, just as Catchpole arrived.

"Not a lot, really, gentlemen. Dean apparently had a decent little house all to himself. I suppose even doing just one or two jobs a year would give him a very good income. There was a load of equipment in his garden workshop, and Barker has shipped it all off to the Yard. The Armourer seemed keen to see how Dean loaded the cartridges and so on. They even found the sawn-off parts from the barrels of the Drilling, so there's no doubt we've found the correct premises.

"What they didn't find was a single scrap of paper in the place. No clue as to where he came from. No sign that anyone else lived with him, and no sign of any visitors, male or female. The nearest neighbours said they saw him perhaps once a month, and had never heard him speak.

"They found another shotgun – a Winchester Model 12 trench gun. That's a pump-action gun. It hadn't been cut down – if it had been, it was surely a more suitable gun for jobs like Wilcox and Cunningham. There was also a Colt automatic pistol. They've both been given to the Armourer to look at. He says that it's possible that the Colt was used for a murder in Nine Elms a few months ago, so he's taking that to Hendon to do some test firing and get the bullets in the comparator microscope.

"All interesting, but not helpful to us, unfortunately.

"Both the weapons found were used extensively by American forces in the last war – and in the Great War too. But they were both produced by the million, and were also used by others outside the US services – I have a Colt, as you know, Sergeant – so we still can't know for sure that Dean was an American.

"I've told Barker to go and see Inspector Lessing, our military liaison officer. He'll talk to the US forces people. Perhaps they can identify the man. Not that his real name really matters to us, I suppose."

Haig passed the post mortem report to the DI, who read it quickly, and shrugged. "Not especially enlightening," he commented.

"No, it isn't," agreed Bryce. "I was lying in bed this morning, mulling things over," he continued. "We assume that Dean must have travelled to Ashton by car. A pretty safe assumption, as he can hardly have come by train – it's five miles from Woodbridge station and lots of locals would have seen him trudging along, both arriving and leaving. So he parks in the wood on the side away from Wilcox's house. Nobody sees him driving around searching for his victim's house, or for a safe location to leave his car. In a place this size I'm sure we'd have heard about anything like that by now. Incidentally, Dean probably hired the car, as they didn't find any sign of one at his place.

"All that said, it seems likely that he had a detailed geographic knowledge of the village. Would you both agree?"

The others nodded.

"Wherever Dean may come from, he isn't a villager – he's a London professional. We have no reason to think that he made a scouting visit earlier. I think that proves that he got his instructions from someone who knows Ashton like the back of his hand. It has to be a resident."

"Surely it doesn't necessarily rule out the Eddingtons, sir?" queried Catchpole. "They may not visit the village very often, but they'd probably know their own wood well enough to know where to get off the road – and they'd have Wilcox's address."

"Yes, good point, but I still put them lower down the list, because I reckon they'd have gone further trying legal methods of voiding the contract, before resorting to murder. Anyway, we three will get over to Ashton; better get a message to Jephson to meet us there.

"We'll split up, at least initially, and each

take one of what we might call the key people. I'll go and see Mrs Redfern. Inspector, you take Mrs Fielding. Sergeant, you talk to the Vicar. Whoever sees Sergeant Jephson when he arrives can tell him to interview the pub landlord.

"I want to know the full extent of the bridge set – the names of any members we haven't yet heard about. Also, the names of anyone else living in the village who might be described as 'middle class', or who might have some money.

"What I'm after now is everything Cunningham did in the weeks *prior* to the first murder. Who did he talk to then? Did he ask any questions during that period, and if so did they pertain in any way to Wilcox?

"When you've extracted what you can from your interviewee, just wander around the village, talking to anyone you happen to meet. Keep an eye on the bench near the shop – we'll meet there after we've all finished, and discuss what's next. With any luck, someone will come up with a new lead!"

***

The church being slightly nearer than the vicarage, Haig looked in there first. The door was unlocked, but inside he found only a pair of cleaners. The women greeted him with interest, and he spent several minutes talking to them. Neither had been interviewed by the police already – and neither had any useful information to impart now. He moved on to the vicarage.

Here he was more successful, as the Vicar himself opened the door.

"Good morning, Sergeant – still going the rounds, then? Do come in."

Mickleburgh escorted his visitor into his study. Papers and books were strewn everywhere – not just on the desk and an adjacent table butting up to it, but on chairs and across the floor as well.

The Vicar, observing Haig's expression, smiled.

"No, Sergeant, I'm not a naturally tidy person. Our maid isn't allowed in here – nor is my wife unless she comes to speak to me. I know where everything is. Once, after the room had been 'tidied', I mislaid an important document that I wanted for preparing a sermon. I found it months later tucked into something else. I can't risk that again. So Audrey and I have reached a compromise. Once a year – on my birthday, actually, to make it easy to remember – the room is tidied and cleaned, under my direct supervision. There's another fortnight to go, so you see it at its most untidy!

"Anyway, can I offer you some refreshment?"

"No, thank you, sir," replied Haig. "This won't take very long, and I'll come straight to the point. As we told you before, we're concentrating on who might have commissioned the assassin to do the job.

"The Suffolk police have seen various

people, as you know, but the Chief Inspector wants to know if there are any more people in the village or nearby with the means to pay such a man – it seems he charged seven hundred and fifty pounds per job."

"Great Scott!" exclaimed the Vicar. "Well, that lets me out – I'm not much better off than the proverbial church mouse. We must catch this person, of course, so let me think.

"I suppose we can split the resident population into three main groups. "First, those in the so-called working class. Land workers, domestic servants, and the like. Most are poor by English standards, and none could possibly dream of ever having the money to pay the fee you mention.

"Then we have those who are better placed, but without being rich. Professionals or retired professionals of one sort or another. Wilcox and Allen were both in that category, of course. Doctor Temple is another. There's a retired naval officer, Rear Admiral Haynes, but he's ninety-seven and more-or-less bedridden. It would be a waste of time trying to interview him – the poor chap has completely lost his memory.

"Not counting Eddington, who doesn't live in the village, there are only three people around here with real money – Mrs Redfern and Mrs Fielding, whom I mentioned yesterday. Then there's Cyril Yardy. He retired to the village about three years ago. Lives in the White House, next door to The Pightle, Wilcox's house. Used to own a factory in the Midlands somewhere, making some sort of machine parts, I understand, but he's not very forthcoming about his past. Doesn't really get involved in the village at all, and it's a bit of a mystery why he and his wife chose to retire here with no connections to the place.

"In no sense am I suggesting he was involved in this, Sergeant – only that he seems to have a lot of money, which he won't spend on my church!"

Haig considered what the Vicar had said, and then asked a supplementary question.

"Another thing is what we might call the bridge circle, sir. We've heard some names from Mrs Fielding and others, but Mr Bryce is interested in getting the full deck, as it were."

"I see," said Mickleburgh. "I expect Christina mentioned the bridge players in Benson's novels?"

"She did, sir."

The Vicar laughed. "She's not wrong in some ways, although the parallels are far from perfect. My wife doesn't squeak, for a start, and I never speak with a *faux* Scottish accent.

"The circle is quite small now. Three prominent members – Hermione Wilcox, Cameron Fielding, and Lawrence Redfern – all died in fairly quick succession. Then George backed out of playing too. The circle, if you can call it that, now consists of Christina and Cynthia, the Temples, Audrey and myself, and a couple of spinster sisters, the Coppingers. We need a hundred percent turnout to get two tables, now.

"Desmond Allen used to play occasionally, but only if we could convince him that we really needed him to make up a four. We've lost him now.

"I tried to get Yardy and his wife interested, but he maintained that they can't play. I'm pretty sure he can, as a matter of fact, as I overheard a conversation on one of his very rare forays into Ashton society, when he spoke knowledgeably about ruffing. I never repeated the invitation, though – it was clear that for some reason the man simply didn't want to join in."

"The Coppingers, sir – can you tell me about them?"

"Blanche and Bridget. Both in their late fifties, I should say. They live in Laburnum Cottage. They don't really fit into any of my three categories – they're from the upper middle class but have very little money. Impoverished gentlefolk, really. Lovely ladies, though, and very sharp card players.

"I must say that I don't see what connection there might be between bridge-playing and murder, Sergeant, but you know your job, I suppose."

After a few more minutes of general conversation about village life, Haig thanked the Vicar for his help, and took his leave.

***

The DCI, meanwhile, had also found Mrs Redfern at home. She was pleased to see him again, and seemed disappointed when he turned down her offer of coffee. Before he could ask his questions, he had to answer her own; she had noted from his card that he was a barrister, and insisted that he told her something of his background. Reluctant, as always, to talk about himself, he squeezed a potted history into two minutes before managing to change the subject.

He learned little, and was given the same three names that Haig was almost simultaneously being given by the Vicar.

Deciding to be open with the lady, he told her about the London gunman and how much he allegedly charged for each 'job'.

"If I'm correct that he was paid by someone here with a grudge, Mrs Redfern, you can see that you are a prime suspect," he said with a smile, to make the observation less stark. "You were annoyed with the first victim. You have the money to pay a professional. I don't suggest that you yourself made the arrangements, but I don't doubt you have loyal retainers who would be only too glad to do that on your behalf."

Cynthia Redfern smiled too. "Oh yes, I expect I have a few who'd be willing to try if I asked them to, Chief Inspector. No doubt you'll look at Wellbeloved, for a start. However, I can't see how the poor chap would manage – I know for a fact that he's never been to London in his life, so he wouldn't know where to start looking for a professional killer.

"The same argument applies to my butler, footman, and gardeners. They're all countrymen, through and through. Apart from war service in a few cases, a trip to Ipswich is the furthest they've ever travelled.

"And that, of course, is on top of the fact that I should never dream of asking any of my employees to break the law in any way. You're on the wrong track with me as your suspect, Chief Inspector."

Bryce was sufficiently convinced by this response to grin. "You may well be right, Mrs Redfern," he replied as he stood up. "Anyway, thank you again for your assistance."

He drove back to the village centre, where he found his Sergeant sitting on the bench. He had barely sat down himself when Jephson drove up, and before he could join the Yard men Catchpole also arrived.

"This bench won't accommodate four, and it's getting chilly," observed the DCI, "let's go and sit in our car."

Bryce and Haig took the front seats, and the Suffolk men sat behind.

There was a brief exchange of information. It was immediately clear that all three men had been given the same three additional names.

Catchpole told his colleagues that Mrs

Fielding had expressed some distaste for Mr Yardy, but he had gained the impression that this was simply because the man chose to ignore the social conventions of the moneyed classes in a village.

Sergeant Jephson said that he had looked through Cunningham's notebooks, back to a month before he took the Ashton cottage.

"There was only one thing remotely helpful in the books, gentlemen. Wilcox's name appeared – without any explanation or comment – just a week before he took on the tenancy.

"Otherwise they're just like his most recent book. Quite detailed notes of every interview, everything he was doing, in fact. But as we've seen, he put down hardly anything about this matter from start to finish. Almost as if he was worried about somebody seeing it."

There was a silence in the car, as the others took this in.

"Well," said the DCI at last, "it does confirm that Cunningham knew something about Wilcox before he went to Ashton, so I suppose we've advanced our investigation a little.

"The only adverse things we know about Wilcox, apart from his short temper, relate to what might be termed fraudulent dealings with property belonging to the two widows. Quite large sums involved, really. If it's one or both of those that Cunningham got a sniff of, then I suppose that would be something for a young reporter to follow up. But where did he learn about it?"

"His mother said she had no idea why he was going to Ashton so often, and couldn't understand it," remarked Catchpole.

"Same with his friend Neville Dearden," said Haig. "But Dearden did mention girlfriends – if we get desperate maybe we should find the most recent and enquire of her. Hopefully she's heard about his death by now," he added as an afterthought.

"Good point, Sergeant. Next time we're by a telephone, call Dearden and see if he has any names. As for Mrs Cunningham. I can't really believe she wouldn't have asked her son the direct question as to why he was taking the Ashton cottage. Surely he must have given some reason?

Bryce swivelled around in his seat to face the officers in the back. "So, Inspector, I want you and Sergeant Jephson to go and see her yet again. Push the point – sensitively, of course, but firmly. You can also enquire about girlfriends.

"We'll continue here. Haig, you take Yardy, who lives in the house next to Wilcox's. That fact may or may not be relevant, but bear it in mind. As the most senior, I'll give myself what's probably the easiest job, and see the Coppinger sisters. When I've done that, I'll see if I can find Mr Sanderson at the pub; might be opening time by then.

"We don't have wireless cars out here to let us pass on what each of us is finding, so I think we'd better meet back at Woodbridge again.

"I'll see you back here in a little while, Haig,

and when we've had a chat you can take Jephson's car back to the station." Jephson tossed his key to Haig, who snatched it deftly out of the air.

The Suffolk officers drove off in Catchpole's car, as the Yard men went off to their respective targets.

CHAPTER 13

Sergeant Haig walked round to The White House. Although not identical to Wilcox's, Cyril Yardy's property was of similar size and built at about the same time, probably by the same builder. He was reaching towards the bell when the door was opened by a large and almost bald man of about fifty.

"Saw you coming up the drive," he said. "You're police, no doubt. No point in wasting my maid's time when it's me you'll want to talk to anyway. My name's Yardy, by the way, but I expect you know that. Come in."

He led Haig into a compact office. The window overlooked the drive, and clearly this was where Yardy had been sitting. Haig introduced himself, and showed his warrant card.

"Take a seat, Sergeant, and tell me what you want from me. You're looking into the murder of Wilcox, of course?"

"Not just him, sir. You may not have heard this yet, but another of your villagers, Mr Allen, has also been shot – as has Mr Cunningham, a reporter who lived here and was investigating for his newspaper."

Yardy looked surprised.

"Hadn't heard about those two. I don't take much interest in the goings on in the village. Knew Wilcox, of course – he lived next door, although I rarely saw him. Met Allen a few times, but had nothing in common with him, so I've nothing useful to tell you there. But Cunningham – yes. He came here a few days ago, asking questions. I spoke to him on the doorstep, wouldn't let him in, even though he said he lived in the village. That was neither here nor there. Don't like reporters. Basically he just wanted to know if I knew anyone who might want to kill Wilcox. Put him straight and told him that was a stupid question – I'd have notified the police if I knew anything. Sent him on his way.

"So, dead is he? Same way as Wilcox?"

"Yes, sir; a sawn-off shotgun, but in his case in Liverpool Street station."

"Good God. Either a madman on the loose, or a professional gunman, then, one assumes. What about Allen?"

"Here in the village, sir. Probably at the same time as Mr Wilcox, it's just that his body wasn't found for a few days. May just have been in the wrong place and saw something."

Yardy grunted.

"I see why you've come to me, Sergeant. Someone paid money – probably a large sum of money if the gunman is any good – and you lot are trawling round to see who could stump up the cash. Not many of us around here who could, probably, and no doubt I'm high up on the list!

"Well, all I can say is this – it wasn't me. I had no quarrel with Wilcox. Even I had, I can't think of any dispute which would be so serious that I'd have considered murdering him. And if there had been something, I'd have sorted it out myself, not gone sneaking off to some hired hitman to do my dirty work.

"As I said, I don't get involved in village matters. I can't tell you anything about who might have been annoyed with Wilcox. Must have been something pretty bad though, one assumes."

Haig agreed that it must have been, and prepared to leave, no further forward than when he arrived.

***

Bryce had an even shorter walk, as Laburnum Cottage was within fifty yards of the village stores. From the outside, it looked like a larger – but much better cared for – version of Cunningham's house. The front garden was well-tended, and still displayed plenty of late autumn colour with fuchsias, nerines, and a particularly large acer. The DCI used the antique brass knocker on the front door and immediately heard twittering voices inside. The door opened to reveal two ladies.

Bryce identified himself, and was immediately invited inside and escorted into the living room. There he was told to sit down in an armchair. Once again he declined the offer of coffee. The two spinsters sat side by side on a small sofa opposite, and introduced themselves as Blanche and Bridget.

Looking at them, it was quite clear they were sisters, although Bryce would have found it difficult to say which was the elder, and wondered if they were twins. Both wore identical white lace high-necked blouses, and black skirts which almost reached the floor. The DCI thought their dress style probably hadn't changed in forty years. Looking at a pair of yellowing photographs on the mantelpiece, each showing a young subaltern, he guessed that both sisters had lost a fiancé in the Great War, and had remained single ever since.

"Please forgive the intrusion ladies," he said. "As you know, we're looking into the murder of George Wilcox – and you may also have heard that Desmond Allen and a reporter named Marcus Cunningham have also been killed."

The sisters twittered to one another again – there was no other word for their bird-like chattering.

"Yes, quite awful, Chief Inspector," said Blanche, "but we really know nothing about any of these things."

Bridget chirruped her agreement. "Murder is such a manly preoccupation and preserve, don't you find, Chief Inspector?"

Bryce could think of many cases of female killers, and in other circumstance would have been prepared to debate the point, but for the sake of expediency he decided not to pursue it.

"No, I don't expect you know anything about this murder, ladies, but you may still be able to help us. You both play bridge, I hear?"

"Oh yes," replied Bridget, "it's a wonderful way for us to keep our brains sharp as we get older, and of course it was a perfect entrée for us into Ashton when we first moved here."

"You're not life-long villagers, then?" asked the DCI.

"Oh no, Chief Inspector, replied Blanche, " we inherited this cottage from an old relative fifteen or so years ago."

Bridget nodded, and chirruped, "Uncle Emmanuel lived with us in our parents' house for a time in the 1920s. It was he who taught us to play bridge as well as we do, actually, and so we were able to slip into the circle here very easily. We played auction bridge first, of course, but it's only contract bridge now.

"George used to play a lot too," she continued, "but he gave up after Hermione passed away."

"Not straight after, dear," corrected Blanche. "He carried on for a few months after that, and *then* he suddenly gave up. One rather suspects that something must have happened, but goodness only knows what it was."

Bridget turned and acknowledged her sister's correction. "Quite right, dearest, quite right." To Bryce she said, "We hardly spoke to him in the last few months, you know."

"I hear he could be a bit difficult when playing cards," remarked Bryce.

A fresh outburst of twittering ensued, after which both sisters spoke almost in unison:

"Very rude, at times!"

"But nothing to make either of us shoot him, Chief Inspector," said Blanche.

"No, of course not," agreed Bryce, "I'm sure there was something rather more than that. Trouble is, we haven't found it yet.

"Please forgive my asking, but we're looking for someone who could afford to pay about fifteen hundred pounds to carry out these murders. Would that be within your means, ladies?"

The Misses Coppinger were much amused by the question. Bridget recovered first.

"Forgive us Chief Inspector – it isn't a laughing matter, of course. But really, it would take us ten years to find such an amount, and it would mean not eating in the meantime! We don't even have a maid. We can only just afford Mrs Webber to come in a couple of times a week to do some heavy cleaning and the laundry for us. We find the copper and the mangle are too much for us now. No, no; you must look elsewhere for your criminal."

"Have you approached that exceedingly strange man Cyril Yardy," suggested Blanche. "He's certainly got more money than he knows what to do with, and he doesn't seem to like anyone in the village. Not that I'm saying he's a murderer," she added quickly.

Bryce sensed that, as he had anticipated, there was nothing to be found in this household, and he rose to leave, confirming as he did so that Mr Yardy was indeed being interviewed.

Both women clucked around him as he walked back to the front door. He said goodbye, and walked thoughtfully back to the bench, on which a very elderly bearded man was now sitting. The DCI put him down as another like Spraggons, probably a long-retired farm worker. The man rose as he approached, and actually pulled his forelock – something which Bryce couldn't recall ever seeing before in real life.

"Do sit down again, please" said the DCI. I'm Chief Inspector Bryce, one of the detectives from London. I'll join you here for a few minutes until my Sergeant comes back, if you don't mind."

"Ar, Henry Pye, I be, zur," said the ancient, "and I know nowt," he added. "Mr Wilcox, he was always polite to me, though, not like some as I could mention. But it's they lah-di-dah women what's mostly rude to the likes of me. Men of the quality, they mostly be more unnerstandin'."

This was an aspect of differences between the sexes which Bryce had not met before, and in other circumstances (as with the Coppingers) he would have been interested in exploring the topic. He contented himself with a few questions about what the villagers were thinking.

It seemed that Pye was aware of the additional deaths, and their circumstances, because he immediately opened up with a question about how much a paid killer might expect to earn. Bryce provided the information, and the old man whistled – or tried to.

"Nice pay, but dirty, dirty, work," he said. "Don't think many'd risk their necks even for that."

It seemed that Mr Pye had never actually spoken to Wilcox. The 'politeness' extended only to either a wordless nod or a raise of the hand from the lawyer when the two passed one another in the village. He knew nothing about Wilcox, either good or bad, and Bryce thought he was telling the truth. The two men chatted briefly about the quality of ale in the Royal Oak, and whether there would ever be another war. The DCI learned that his companion had been too old to be called up in the Great War, and was one of those Mrs Redfern had mentioned who had never set foot outside Suffolk. Born in 1868, he had worked for the Redferns since 1881, and again Bryce would have liked to spend some time with the old man, learning something of how the way of life changed over that time – if indeed it had changed much at all in this little backwater.

Haig's return ended the conversation, and

the old man wandered off, again tugging his forelock to the DCI but not (as Bryce noted in silent amusement) to the Sergeant.

Haig grinned as Pye shuffled off. "I didn't even need to speak for him to know I'm not officer material, sir!"

Bryce laughed. "Touching one's cap is quite common, of course, and even touching the forehead when no cap is being worn. But it's the first time I've seen a genuine tug of the forelock.

"How did you find Mr Yardy?"

"Co-operative but uninformative, sir. Says he didn't know about the deaths apart from Wilcox's. Takes little interest in the village, apparently.

"He's sharp though; as soon as I'd mentioned the sawn-off shotgun he realised it must be a professional gunman, and concluded we're looking for someone with the means to pay for one. Says he didn't really know Wilcox, even though they were next-door neighbours. Not the sort of man who socialises, I suppose. I didn't see a wife. What about you, sir?"

"A pair of elderly spinsters. Lived together all their lives, and think and sometimes speak almost as one. Very good card players, I was told, but I'd never have guessed that in talking to them today. Hidden depths, perhaps, but not so deep as to be closet murderers, I think. Clearly don't have two groats between them, so no question of Dean being on their payroll.

"It's opening time, Sergeant. Let's get a bite to eat in the Oak."

In the pub, they found the landlord polishing some horse brasses. The man quickly deduced who his customers were, and after shouting their food orders to someone in the kitchen, he drew their pints of bitter shandy, and said:

"Janey told me you might want to ask questions, gentlemen. You'll want to hear what I know about these killings. Simple answer is nothing. Matter of fact, I've lost three customers. Mr Allen was a regular – his own pint pot hangs in the bar. Mr Wilcox used to come in often too, although we hadn't seen him in a while. The reporter lad used to come in now and then, when he was staying here – he sometimes ate here of an evening, as well."

"We're interested in what he might have talked about, Mr Sanderson," said Haig. "Not necessarily to you, but in a conversation you might have heard with anyone else in the bar. Did he ask questions, for instance?"

The landlord paused to think. "I remember soon after he first come, he asked me to give him an outline of who lived in the village. Just the quality, mind, he wasn't interested in most people. He said he'd moved into the village, and I thought he just wanted to meet some people. I didn't know then where he was living, and at the time had no idea he was a reporter, so I suppose I gave him a picture of the people who might be his sort. I never asked what he did for a living; I thought he was probably an author or something, come for a bit of peace and quiet to write his books.

"After that, we spoke occasionally when he came in the pub, but he never asked me any more questions. It was only after the murder that he told people about his job, and started striding around with his notebook."

"You say Mr Wilcox used to be a regular – did you ever see him and Mr Cunningham in here talking together?" asked the DCI.

"Can't say as I did, sir. But thinking back, I reckon Mr Wilcox had stopped coming in here a little before Mr Cunningham arrived in Ashton." The kitchen door opened.

"Now, here's your food coming, gentlemen."

The two men enjoyed another basic but satisfying ploughman's lunch, saying very little as they ate. Both were feeling slightly despondent, thinking that the case wasn't moving forward very well.

Their meal finished, Bryce said, "You take Jephson's car back to Woodbridge. I'll see you there – I just want to take a quick look at the church first."

Haig drove off, and the DCI walked through the rather dilapidated lych gate into the churchyard. He wandered through the graveyard, and appraised the church from various angles. As he walked between the tombstones, he was reminded of Haig's comment – that the inscriptions on old gravestones were often so worn away as to be indecipherable. There were a number in that condition here, and he imagined that some might have been standing for well over five hundred years.

He came to an area with more recent monuments. Here, many of the inscriptions were still bright and clear. He glanced at some as he passed, appreciating the local history that many names represented. 'Finbow' was, he believed, a contraction of the name Finborough, another Suffolk village. 'Kerridge', he seemed to recall, was a more modern spelling of a name mentioned in the Domesday Book.

Suddenly he stopped, looking back to a headstone he had just passed. He bent down and studied this particular stone for some time, lost in concentration.

At last, he straightened up, and went to see if the Vicar was in the church. Finding the building empty, he moved on to the vicarage and knocked on the door. As for Haig earlier, it was opened by the Vicar in person.

"My goodness, Chief Inspector, I must really be under suspicion. I've not long said goodbye to your Sergeant. Will you come in?"

"I won't, thank you, Vicar. I've been looking round your churchyard, and I'd like to take a quick look at some of the parish registers, if I may. Are they kept in the church?"

"Yes; it's quite dry in the vestry, so they can safely be stored there. They're locked in a cupboard. Although the church is very old, the number of entries each year isn't huge, of course. Even so, I suppose one day the registers will have to be moved to somewhere more suitable. The earliest are probably in some danger after all these years. Anyway, come along and I'll unlock the cupboard for you."

As they walked back to the church, the Vicar remarked, "You're only the second person to look at the registers since I've been the incumbent here. Apparently the reporter, Cunningham, asked to see them a week or so ago."

Bryce stopped and turned towards the Vicar in astonishment.

"What? Why ever didn't you mention that before?"

Mickleburgh was taken aback by the force of the Chief Inspector's reaction. He blinked in surprise and defended himself. "Well, I only learned about it over breakfast this morning. When he came to ask to see the registers, I was out, and my wife brought him over here as I am doing with you. She unlocked the cupboard, and left him. He agreed to lock up after himself, and return the cupboard key to the vicarage when he'd finished.

"Apparently, he was back with the key within half an hour, and Audrey never thought any more about it. It was only this morning that she mentioned it to me, and I admit that I was thinking of something else at the time and didn't attach any importance to what she was saying."

"Well, I don't expect to be any longer than that myself, Mr Mickleburgh. I'll return the key to the vicarage."

"You needn't go to the trouble, Chief Inspector. I have a few things to attend to while I'm here, so I'll wait."

Entering the vestry, the Vicar unlocked a large cupboard, revealing a number of books of varying ages.

"Anything in particular, Chief Inspector?"

"The baptismal register since 1900, please."

The Vicar selected a volume, and placed it on the vestry table. "All yours, Chief Inspector," he said; "I'll go and see to something else."

Bryce sat down and opened the register. Turning the pages, he saw, as the Vicar had said, that there really weren't many entries. He scanned each page as he turned. Coming to a particular entry, he stopped. After looking at this for a long minute, he closed the register again, replaced it on its shelf, and as the Vicar had left the key in the lock, relocked the cupboard and removed the key.

He returned to the nave and found the cleric at the lectern, tucking slips of paper into the huge bible to mark the sources of the lessons at the next service.

"Thank you, Vicar," he said, handing over the key. "I've seen all I need."

Mickleburgh didn't seem at all curious, and

asked no questions.

The DCI returned to the green, and walked over to the cottage next door to Cunningham's. He tapped on the door. The old occupant opened it, and didn't seem surprised to see the police officer again.

"Just a few more questions for you, Mr Spraggons. I expect your memory is pretty good, but perhaps five bob might improve it some more?"

Spraggons produced an almost toothless smile.

"Oi remembers pretty well, sir; it's the old bones that are giving me bother, not me brain." Bryce was treated to another gum-filled grin. "But 'tis true the brain might work even better when me palm is crossed wi' silver!"

Bryce laughed. He asked three questions, and the old man was able to answer each. The DCI produced two half-crowns, and handed them over.

"One very important thing, Mr Spraggons. Don't mention to anyone – no one at all – what we've talked about. Bear in mind Mr Cunningham was killed; and I rather think that was because he found out what you've just told me. I wouldn't want you to tempt fate the same way."

"Oi'm not so green as Oi'm cabbage-looking," replied the old boy. "Oi'll not be speaking out o' turn."

CHAPTER 14

The DCI drove back to Woodbridge police station.

"See if you can rustle up a couple of teas, please Sergeant," he said to the desk man as he passed through the foyer.

He joined Haig in the little office. "There's some tea coming, he announced. "We'll wait for that to arrive before getting down to business." He then sat silent for five minutes, looking into space.

With the arrival of the Constable bringing the tea, Bryce seemed to return to earth.

"I was very lucky today," he said, as the door closed again. "As I walked through the churchyard, I looked at various gravestones – including some like you described, the inscriptions completely illegible. And then I saw one headstone which was only twenty or so years old, with the writing as clear as the day it was put there:

"*Wesley Winterbourne Johnson, beloved husband of Christina, and father of James.*"

"Johnson – you mean like the soldier who shot Dean? But he's Reginald."

"Yes. So I then went to the church, and

looked at the registers. The infant son of Wesley and Christina Johnson was baptised with the names James Reginald.

"I then had another chat with old Spraggons. He confirms that the Johnsons had a son. Jimmy, he was known as. It seems he was always a bit odd, and there was some trouble more than once. Spraggons thinks he was once expelled from school for stealing.

"In early 1929, his father died, and that same year Mrs Fielding – Johnson as she was then – took James to visit her own father who lived in Italy. She and the boy – who would have been about nine – were apparently intending to remain with the grandfather for the rest of the summer.

"According to Spraggons – who may be aged but definitely has all his marbles – the boy died in a boating accident. His body was never recovered. After a while Mrs Johnson came home – and of course there was no body to bring back, even if such arrangements could have been made. Spraggons said that when she got back, her maids passed the information around the village that she didn't want to discuss her loss with anyone.

"That was over twenty years ago. It seems it was the talk of the village for a few weeks, and then the topic just faded into oblivion. The present Vicar and the Doctor never knew James, and probably have never even known of his existence. Same for Yardy. Even the Coppingers moved here after the boy disappeared. As Inspector Catchpole told us, young people haven't stayed in the village. Probably his contemporaries have all gone. Of course, Mrs Redfern must have known of him, and Wilcox and Allen might have remembered him too, I suppose, but that's probably irrelevant."

"So your theory is that the boating accident might have been untrue, sir, and that James is still alive?"

"Well, I know it seems an unlikely story, and there are certainly a lot of gaps in it, but yes. It's the name, you see. Johnson isn't uncommon, of course, but the coincidence of a Reginald Johnson. He would be about the right age to be the Liverpool Street soldier...and his mother had a grudge against Wilcox."

"But James was only a child back then, sir! What happened for the next few years?"

"I guess his grandfather looked after him. The next bit in Spraggons' story is that within a matter of months Mrs Johnson married Cameron Fielding. I don't know whether he was aware that his wife had borne a child, but Fielding wasn't a local man and, as far as we know, had never seen the boy."

Haig took some time to turn all this over in his mind. "You're thinking that Mrs Fielding and her father might have conspired to conceal from the new husband the existence of what may have been a very troubled child?"

"Perhaps, yes. Then, at some point when James was older, maybe when war was imminent, he returned to England but still never came back to Ashton. My theory is tenuous, I know, but I suspect that his mother has always been in contact with him, and possibly financed him. She is apparently wealthy in her own right, regardless of what her second husband might have had. We don't know what happened to the grandfather, of course – if he died there may have been even more money."

Haig gave all this some more thought, and then raised two objections.

"But if it was him at Liverpool Street, where did he get the army uniform? And why on earth would he give the City police his real name?"

"I'll give my theoretical answer to your second question first. It was a tremendous risk, of course, but I think he had to admit his name. He couldn't know that they wouldn't ask to see his ID. He may have had army papers, or he may have only had a civilian ID card – but either way he couldn't risk giving a false name. He did use the 'Reginald' name though – perhaps so that if the matter was reported in the press the name Reginald Johnson wouldn't be likely to mean anything to anyone in Ashton. But in any case, Playford told us that Johnson asked for his name to be suppressed at the inquest.

"As for the uniform, there seem to be three possibilities. Maybe he hired it from a theatrical costumier, and managed to get hold of a suitable pistol. Or he could be a genuine serving officer, although I think that's extremely unlikely. My hunch is that he was actually in the army at some point, and retained his uniform and pistol.

"As we know, he somehow overcame the first enormous risk, but he must have known there were two other huge problems looming up. It was inevitable that he would be summoned to give evidence at both inquests, probably in a matter of days rather than weeks – and when that happened the army in Colchester would deny his existence, and suspicions would arise. I didn't pay much attention at the time, but Mr Playford mentioned that Johnson had said he was about to leave the army, and would contact the police with his new address. I've no idea what Johnson was going to do next; he might have been planning to disappear completely – no doubt with financial aid from his mother.

"Anyway, everything is pointing to him now."

Haig nodded slowly. "How are you going to play this, sir?"

"We could bring Mrs Fielding in on suspicion, and search her house to find Johnson's address. Or we could put out an alert for him, and try to locate him that way.

"But first of all we'll contact the military liaison officer, and see if Johnson actually served in the army at all.

"If he didn't, then we'll try the costumiers. We'll discuss how to deal with Mrs Fielding when the Inspector gets back."

Bryce picked up the telephone, and gave the Scotland Yard number. When he was connected, he asked for Inspector Lessing.

"Hello, Stephen," he said. "I'm still on the double shooting in London, linked to two more murders in Suffolk. It seems I've been asking for your help in almost every one of my cases lately, and this is the second time in this one.

"I need to know now about James Reginald Johnson, born fourth of February, nineteen twenty. Look first at the Royal Norfolks, and widen the net if that fails. I'm at Woodbridge police station."

After a bit of chat between the two friends, Bryce asked the Inspector to return him to the Yard switchboard so he could speak to DC Barker. He instructed the detective to go to Records and see if anything was known about Johnson. Replacing the receiver, he turned to Haig.

"Mr Lessing is going to check – says it won't take long. He also reports that there is no Abe Dean. The Americans think our gunman may be Private First Class Alvin ('Al') Sullivan, who deserted in 1944 and has been missing ever since. The photograph seems to correspond with their records, but they're doing more checks.

"As you heard, I'm getting Barker to see if anything is known about Johnson in civilian life.

"Something else, Sergeant. It seems Cunningham went to look at the church registers shortly before he was killed. Pound to a penny he found what I did in the churchyard – and he was either seen. or he mentioned the son's existence to someone.

"I think we can rule the Vicar out. Until this morning he didn't know Cunningham had been looking at the records – apparently it was Mrs Mickleburgh who gave him access to the registers. She probably didn't know what he was looking for. And today the Vicar himself was completely incurious too.

"However, I guess that Cunningham then spoke to someone – as I did to Spraggons today – and that got back to Mrs Fielding somehow. One of her servants, perhaps. Or maybe she just happened to see Cunningham enter the church with Mrs Mickleburgh, and put two and two together.

"He very probably didn't harbour any suspicions about Johnson – it may be that he was just curious about this son that nobody ever mentioned. If he did have suspicions, one would think that he'd have been a bit more careful about going alone to meet an informant in London."

"I hope Spraggons doesn't say anything, sir."

"I'm sure he won't. I told him that Cunningham had been shot after he learned the same fact, and the old boy got the point. He's far from daft, he told me!"

Haig was thinking again. "Isn't it possible that even if the accidental death was faked, the young Johnson might really be dead now, sir – killed in the war, perhaps – and someone has assumed his identity?"

"Quite possible, and if so my theory bites the dust. It won't be the first time I've been barking up the wrong tree, as you'll remember. But this time I'm happy to put all my eggs in the one basket – at least for the moment."

The telephone rang, and Bryce picked up the handset. He was surprised to hear the Liaison Officer again so soon. He listened closely to what his caller had to say, thanked him for the remarkably quick service, and put the receiver down again. He looked at Haig.

"A James Reginald Johnson, with the birthday stated, was commissioned into the Royal Norfolk Regiment in 1940. He doesn't seem to have done anything useful, and never served overseas. It would appear he was unsatisfactory. The army didn't use the RAF term 'lack of moral fibre', but a couple of comments on his record suggest much the same thing. In 1944 he was accused of theft, and cashiered after a court martial. For some reason he avoided the glasshouse, and after his discharge everyone seems to have forgotten him. Some in those circumstances were sent to serve in the coal mines, but perhaps he wasn't suitable for that either.

"I think there's little doubt this is our man."

***

The sound of footsteps in the corridor presaged

the return of Catchpole and Jephson.

"No joy at all, sir," reported the Inspector, as he pulled up a chair. "We talked to Mrs Cunningham. She knew of no connection between her son and the village of Ashton. No friend that she knew of who might have lived there either. She appreciates that there must have been some reason to make him lease his 'hovel' there, but when she queried it – more than once – he just brushed the question aside. She knows he has had the odd girlfriend, but she had no knowledge of a current one."

Catchpole spread his hands. "Dead loss, I'm afraid, sir."

Bryce grinned. "All is not lost. Tell him the news, Sergeant."

Haig efficiently summarised what had been happening, and the two Suffolk men goggled at him as he spoke.

"Blimey, sir, you've got it sorted again!" exclaimed Catchpole.

"Hopefully, but very fortuitously though. If I hadn't gone for a walk through the churchyard, and if I hadn't happened to spot that gravestone, I think we'd have been struggling, perhaps to the point of giving up.

"Something else has come to me. Hindsight is a wonderful thing. I don't suppose I would have twigged this either, but Mr Playford didn't note something that was probably staring him in the face. Johnson appeared in the uniform of an army officer. Whether or not he still had army papers, there are three discrepancies in his presentation.

"First, he is of an age where he could have joined the army at or soon after the start of the war. Yet now, nearly ten years on, he is still only a lieutenant. That's very, very unlikely, although I suppose he might have recently been commissioned from the ranks.

"Second, and we'll need to confirm this with Mr Playford, I bet he wasn't wearing decorations. He should, at the very least, have had the basic service ribbons. The 1939-45 War medal, for a start – you only needed twenty-eight days of service in uniform to qualify for that one.

"Third, and again I'd need to check on this, I don't think army officers routinely carry sidearms four years after the war. I don't, as a reservist."

The others were still taking that in when the telephone rang again. Haig, who was nearest to the instrument, picked it up. He made some notes on a pad as he listened.

"Very good, Barker, well done. I'll tell the DCI." He rang off, and turned to the others.

"Johnson has a record, sir. Nothing known prior to 1945, but convicted three times since then – three offences of dishonesty, and one of common assault. Fined the first time for a petty theft, then three sentences of imprisonment – three months, four months, and six months.

"We have an address as of early this year – 45C Holls Lane, N4. Not a million miles from Dean

– or Sullivan, or whatever his name was."

"Excellent," said the DCI. "We'll pick him up and get him brought to Woodbridge. Sergeant, get on to Barker again. Tell him to find another DC – Kittow if he's available – and then liaise with the Islington DDI to get Johnson arrested on my authority – suspicion of the murder of Sullivan at Liverpool Street will do for a start. Emphasise that at least one experienced officer should be armed when going to make the arrest. Barker and Kittow can caution Johnson and bring him here."

Haig picked up the telephone, and Bryce continued:

"So far, Inspector, we don't have any evidence against Mrs Fielding. However, I think we have enough to apply for a search warrant. Would you like to go and see a local JP and swear an information? If he agrees to issue a warrant, all four of us will go and search the house. If we find anything to prove she's in contact with her son we can consider arresting her."

Catchpole nodded, and left the room.

Haig was busy on the telephone.

"Yes, if the DDI wants to check with Mr Bryce, he can call him here. Yes, they know each other, and I think it's very unlikely…No, get DC Kittow to draw a pistol from the armoury – he's cleared to carry firearms now…Well, if the Armourer wants Mr Bryce's authority he'll have to ring us here…Yes, I assume Islington will send a ranking officer on the raid, but as far as you're concerned you do as Kittow says. And someone needs to search Johnson's premises. We want the gun, for a start, and the uniform, and any papers which show a link to his mother. Understand? Right, just get on with it, man!"

An exasperated Haig slammed down the phone. Bryce and Jephson looked amused.

"Sorry, sir, I suppose I can't blame Barker, but he seemed to be thinking of every possible problem."

"So we gathered. I'm glad you told him to take instructions from Kittow – a cooler head. I expect the local DDI will take charge himself, but the last thing you want is indecision during a raid where the target not only has a gun but has killed already."

The telephone rang again. Haig listened, then passed the receiver to Bryce. "The Armourer, sir."

"Hallo Freddie...Yes, quite correct...I can hardly give you a signed chitty when I'm in the wilds of rural Suffolk, but I'm giving you this instruction in the presence of two detective sergeants. Just give Kittow whatever he's happy with – he's qualified and capable, as you know...Thanks, Freddie; I'll sign your paperwork tomorrow, probably, and buy you a pint."

He replaced the receiver again.

"That's all in hand. Just a matter of waiting, now, to see if your DI is granted the warrant, Jephson. Since we've got a bit of time to kill, tell us what life's like in the Suffolk CID."

The local DS was happy to oblige. "Well, sir, two murder cases inside six months is quite a bit above the county average, so it's been all go lately. I'm looking forward to the Felixstowe case getting to court – it'll be my first experience of the Assizes. But when that's over, and this case too, I'll be glad to go back to routine work.

"By the way, sir, if we pin this on Johnson, where do you think he'll be tried?"

"Good question. I hadn't given it any thought. If we charge him with the shooting in Liverpool Street, he'll certainly come up at the Old Bailey. He won't be indicted for more than one murder at a time anyway. If he were to get away with that one somehow, he could certainly be charged over the deaths of Wilcox and Cunningham. I suppose those trials would be held at the Suffolk Assizes.

"If we manage to charge Mrs Fielding, that will definitely be a Suffolk matter. I hope we can find enough evidence – it seems to me that she must have been the initiator of all this."

"Why do you think Johnson turned on Sullivan, sir?" asked Haig.

"I don't know, and it's one of the questions I'll be putting to him. Maybe he simply decided that he didn't want anyone alive to know what had been arranged between them. But the risk he took was so great that I don't think that was the reason. Most likely Sullivan was trying to extract more money – blackmail, effectively."

"Why do you think he picked Liverpool Street to finish off his hireling, sir?" asked Jephson. "Why wouldn't he wait until he could get the man down a dark alley somewhere, with nobody around to be a witness?"

"I haven't asked myself that question, but now you've raised it, I think the answer has to be that he wanted to wait until the gunman had done the Cunningham job before eliminating him. Maybe Johnson thought it wouldn't be too easy to get his hired gun to agree to meet up somewhere else later.

"I think we'll also have to see the young woman who witnessed Sullivan's death. She's probably a genuine bystander, but we still have to consider that she may have been placed there to bear false witness to what he did."

The three officers sat in silence for a while. Before anyone spoke again Catchpole returned, a uniformed constable behind him.

"I've got a warrant from Mr Rudd who lives just round the corner, sir, no problem. Thought we'd take PC Farrell as well, in case we want to leave someone on site, or need an escort to the station."

"Good thinking – welcome, Farrell. I'm DCI Bryce, and this is DS Haig. When we arrive, you and Farrell go round to the back door, Haig, and we three will take the front. We'd better take both your cars, Inspector, plus ours.

"Let's go."

CHAPTER 15

Three police cars pulled up on the green at Ashton. The five officers approached Strickland House, and split up as the DCI had instructed. Catchpole rang the bell. A maid opened the door, and Bryce crisply told her, "Police; stand aside."

Catchpole went to look for a study, as the most likely room where papers might be found.

"Get to the back door and let the others in, Jephson, unless they've managed that already."

Turning to the shaking maid, he asked, "Is your mistress at home?"

Receiving a frightened nod, he said, "Please find her, and tell her the police are here."

Before the girl could move, Mrs Fielding came down the stairs.

"All right, Edna, you go back to the kitchen. What's all this, Chief Inspector?"

"I think you know what it's all about, Mrs Fielding. We have a warrant to search this house."

"I see. I assume other policemen are doing that as we speak. You'd better come and sit down."

She turned, and led the way into the

drawing room, and indicated he should sit in an armchair beside the fireplace. She took the seat opposite, and looked at him calmly.

Before either could speak again, Haig appeared in the doorway. He looked at the DCI and raised an eyebrow.

"Leave the local men to do the search, Sergeant. Come and take notes."

Mrs Fielding affixed Bryce with an enquiring look.

"Will you enlighten me as to what you hope to find here?"

"Certainly, Mrs Fielding. As we speak, Metropolitan police officers are arresting your son, James. When they find him, he will be taken into custody on suspicion of the murder of a professional gunman who went by the name of Abe Dean – although it appears his real name is Alvin Sullivan. There will no doubt be other charges later, relating to the murders of George Wilcox and Marcus Cunningham.

"I confidently expect that you will also be charged with those two murders."

Mrs Fielding sat impassively throughout Bryce's statement. Her response, when it came, was calm.

"I see. I suppose I'd better think about getting a solicitor."

"Yes," replied Bryce, and I think we'd better caution you formally. Sergeant…"

This formality was completed just as

Catchpole tapped at the door and poked his head into the room. He motioned the DCI to come outside. In the hallway, he smiled, and said quietly, "Plenty of good material, sir; so good I can hardly believe it. She's kept dozens of letters from Johnson, including some very recent – and very incriminating – ones. I obviously haven't had time to go through them all, but there are written discussions about getting rid of Wilcox, where Johnson refers to suggestions in his mother's previous letters to him.

"Also, the counterfoils in her cheque book show regular payments to her son, and very recently some much larger sums. Her address book has the same address for Johnson as the Met records show."

"Excellent. I suggest you collect up the most obvious evidence, and then have Jephson go through everything else.

"I'll see what she has to say. Join us as soon as you've arranged that, and bring Farrell in too. You should make the arrest – suspicion of being an accessory before the fact for an act of murder will do."

Bryce returned to the drawing room, where – to his astonishment – he found Mrs Fielding and Haig talking about gardening.

"Your Sergeant is knowledgeable about roses, Chief Inspector, but now you're back I expect you'll want to change the subject."

"He's also very good on cricket and railways,

Mrs Fielding," replied the DCI, feeling able to relax slightly, now definite evidence had been found. "He has to be, in order to work with me. I wasn't aware that gardening might be another topic of mutual interest. That's certainly a possibility. Not roses, though – I'm not very keen on them.

"Do you want to talk to us about your part in the deaths of Messrs Wilcox and Cunningham?"

"Not, I think, until I've spoken with my solicitor."

"As you wish. In a minute, Inspector Catchpole will arrest you, and you'll be taken to Woodbridge police station. You son will be brought there too, when we pick him up."

"I see," said Mrs Fielding, still perfectly calm. "I'd like someone to contact Duncan Congreve. I'm sure he has a solicitor in his firm who undertakes criminal work, but if not he'll no doubt able to recommend someone else."

"I'll see to that myself, Mrs Fielding," said Bryce as Catchpole came into the room, with the uniformed PC behind him.

"Mrs Fielding wants to see a solicitor before saying anything, Inspector, and I'll arrange one for her. Carry out the formal arrest, please, and then you and Farrell take her to Woodbridge. She's been cautioned.

"We'll stay with Sergeant Jephson for a bit."

Catchpole looked at the woman. "I am arresting you on suspicion of being an accessory before the fact to an act of murder.

"Bring her out to my car, Farrell. There's no need for handcuffs," he told the Constable.

The policemen departed with their prisoner, and the DCI explained to his Sergeant what the Inspector had found.

"Cast iron, then is it, sir?" asked Haig as they walked along the corridor to find Jephson.

"I haven't seen the material myself, but Mr Catchpole seems to think it's good enough."

As the two men joined Jephson in Mrs Fielding's study, Haig asked a further question:

"I've seen cases where someone is an accessory 'after' the fact, sir, but I've not come across 'before'. Isn't that conspiracy?"

"Not the same, no. It's covered in the 1861 Offences Against The Person Act. Basically, someone convicted of being an accessory before the fact is liable to the same punishment as someone carrying out the substantive crime.

"There is a lesser offence in the same statute, conspiring or soliciting to commit murder, intended for cases where the murder doesn't actually happen. That carries a sentence of ten years, I think."

"So she'll hang, then, sir?" asked Jephson.

"She'll face the death penalty if convicted, yes. Whether she then gets reprieved may depend on what the letters say about the interaction between her and Johnson. If her son was stupid enough to retain his mother's letters, there may be something there to count against her.

"If the correspondence shows that she positively urged him to kill Wilcox, against whom she had a genuine grievance, that's one thing. It's not an excuse for murder, of course, but her barrister would certainly offer it in mitigation. But killing Cunningham is another matter – if she also pushed her son to do that one, I think that would be the end.

"Inspector Catchpole says that money was paid. If so, that looks like more than just mentioning to her son about what Wilcox did, and Johnson then deciding to act on his own initiative. We'll have to see if Johnson kept any of her letters to know that, though, as I doubt whether either of them will tell us."

Bryce picked up the telephone in the study, and asked to be connected with Congreve's firm. Within a couple of minutes he was able to speak to Mr Congreve. The DCI explained the situation to the obviously shocked lawyer. Congreve confirmed that the firm could offer Lucas Waring as defence solicitor for Mrs Fielding, and that he would arrange for Waring to go to Woodbridge as soon as practicable.

Bryce put down the receiver, and turned to Jephson:

"If you're happy to carry on here, Sergeant, we'll leave you to it. You've got your own car, so we'll see you back at the station in due course."

Outside the house, Bryce indicated that Haig should take the wheel. "You drive back to the station, Sergeant – I want to close my eyes for a few minutes. Please don't talk about roses!"

Haig grinned, and put the engine into gear.

CHAPTER 16

At the police station there was news. Inspector Catchpole was standing by the front desk talking to the Custody Sergeant. He turned to the Yard officers as they came through the door.

"She's booked in, sir. Behaving like she doesn't have a care in the world. I've heard of the 'stiff upper lip', but she takes it to extremes. Wanted to chatter all the way back about gardening – compost, slugs, parsley seed." He shook his head.

"More important, though, they've arrested Johnson without any trouble. Wasn't at his flat, so they kept watch. Within half an hour they picked him up on the street as he was walking home.

"Anything found?" asked Bryce.

"No pistol or army uniform – he obviously ditched those sharpish. But there are some letters from Mrs Fielding – your men are bringing those, along with Johnson. They're expected here in about two hours. The local boys are continuing the search of the flat, and will ask around about what might be known. The Divisional Detective

Inspector, a Mr Pettit, apparently says he owes you, and is very keen to help."

"Good," said the DCI. "Mrs Fielding's Solicitor will be arriving soon, Sergeant," he informed the Custody Officer, "and he'll need some time with his client. That's a Mr Waring, by the way. No doubt you can find a room for them to talk.

"It's already late, and I'm hungry. I'd just like a quick look at the letters from Johnson to his mother, and then I suggest we go and eat, after which we should be able to see Mrs F. It may be that we'll leave Johnson until the morning."

The three officers walked along to their room, and Catchpole produced a dozen or more folders, each bulging with letters.

"Only letters, Inspector – no envelopes?" asked the DCI as he glanced in one of the folders.

"That's right, sir. The earliest dates to long before the war – from when he was first left in Italy. It looks as though she's kept every one since. The most recent – and relevant – ones for us are at the top of the pile. He pushed three letters across the table to the DCI.

Bryce read them through quickly, and then passed them to Haig, who whistled as he read a particular line.

"Pretty clear he's accepting her suggestion regarding Wilcox, anyway."

"Yes; it'll be nice if we can see what she wrote to him, but as you say, these do a pretty good job of damning her."

Sergeant Jephson arrived at that moment, and Bryce signalled Haig to pass the letters to him. Jephson didn't whistle like his fellow-sergeant, but a grin spread from ear to ear as he read.

"Got her, then!" he exclaimed.

"Looks like it. Let's go and eat – I hope you'll join us this time, Sergeant – you missed out before."

Jephson agreed with thanks, and the four officers walked to the Bull.

***

After another decent meal, during which the case wasn't mentioned once, the four returned to the police station. The Desk Sergeant informed them that Mr Waring had been with his client for over half an hour, but that the carload from London had still not arrived.

Bryce nodded. "Stick your head in the door, Sergeant, and enquire if the lawyer wants to speak to the police now, or wait until the morning."

A few seconds later they learned that Mr Waring and his client were ready.

"Bring them along to our room, please. I doubt if your interview room can take six of us."

"Right you are, sir – and I'll bring you an extra chair."

A few minutes later, Lucas Waring arrived with Mrs Fielding. The Solicitor hadn't met any of the four police officers before, and Bryce performed the introductions. Waring and his client sat down on one side of the table, with Bryce and Catchpole opposite. Each sergeant sat next to his officer, but outside the perimeter of the small table. Mrs Fielding still appeared completely composed – her representative less so. The DCI opened the proceedings.

"I remind you that you remain under caution, Mrs Fielding. We're here to talk about the deaths of George Wilcox, Marcus Cunningham, and Alvin Sullivan, also known as Abe Dean. There is Desmond Allen as well, but as far as you're concerned I intend to deal only with the first three for now. I'll tell you what I think happened, and you put me right if I go wrong."

The DCI sat back in his chair, crossing his arms and legs. In a relaxed and conversational tone he set out his hypothesis.

"As far as the people in your village are concerned, your son James was assumed dead, the result of an accident while on holiday in Italy. You never spoke about him after that, and the other villagers who were resident at that time soon realised that you didn't want him mentioned.

"He hadn't been seen in Ashton since he was about nine, and as time went on, fewer and fewer people even knew of his existence. The Vicar and the Doctor, for example, and the Coppingers – even the postmistress – all arrived in the village after he had supposedly died. No doubt if he had any childhood friends in the village they gradually moved away – or perhaps even died in the war.

"I admit my crystal ball is blurred – we don't know where he was or how he survived in the eight or so years before the war came. We do know he had a grandfather, so perhaps James lived with him.

"Nor do we know why you pretended your son had died. I surmise that it was so that you, recently widowed, could marry again unencumbered, as it were – and it seems James was a somewhat troubled child.

"But those gaps in our knowledge are irrelevant. The key point is that you maintained contact with him all that time, and supported him financially."

Bryce paused to assess any reaction from Mrs Fielding, his grey eyes looking into her black ones. Beyond the tiniest flicker of a smile from the coral-coloured lips, Mrs Fielding gave no indication that she was even listening.

The DCI continued. "Quite recently, you had reason to be annoyed with Mr Wilcox. You passed this information on to your son. From reading his replies to you, it's clear that he agreed to your suggestion to eliminate Wilcox. It seems, incidentally, that James was foolish enough to retain some of your letters to him. When he arrives here I expect we'll be able to see the whole sorry picture.

"As far as the murder of Wilcox is concerned, there is ample evidence already to prove that you are an 'accessory before the fact'. As I'm sure Mr Waring has explained, that means you face the same penalty as the person who carries out the crime. I hope you comprehend that?"

The Solicitor shifted uncomfortably in his seat, his expression grave.

"There is also mention of Cunningham in your son's most recent letter, and I think – even without corroboration from anything James has retained – there will be enough to prove that you are an accessory in that matter too," said Bryce, his eyes still locked on Mrs Fielding's face. He paused again.

Waring shifted again and looked even more uncomfortable as his client began to speak.

"Bravo, Chief Inspector. I really can't fault your summary. As you say, your 'gaps' may not be relevant, but before going any further I'll fill them in for you anyway. My father, from whom I was – thanks to my wretched mother – completely estranged, was an Italian, living in Salerno. I knew nothing about him, as mother had always refused to have his name mentioned. When she died in 1929, I found details about him among her papers. But before I could do anything more, my husband – James' father – died quite unexpectedly, only a few weeks later. Soon after Desmond's funeral I managed to make contact with my father. It was agreed that James and I would go to stay with him that summer. At that time I knew nothing about him, but I found that he lived extremely well – and that his English was near perfect.

"A couple of days before our journey, while James was still away at school, I was on a train coming back from a concert in London. The first time I'd been to any function since I was widowed, incidentally. There was only one other person in my compartment – Cameron Fielding. I learned that he detested London, but had travelled that day to attend a memorial service for some old friend. I also learned that he was a bachelor. He was travelling on to Norwich, where he lived, but in the hour and a half we were together I fell in love with him, and I thought he seemed to reciprocate that feeling. We arranged to meet when I returned from holiday. However, I foresaw an impediment. While a second husband might – unlike a lion – with some degree of reluctance accept another man's child, the fact was that James was a very difficult character. I thought that might sway Cameron's decision and turn him away from me.

"It was a problem which preoccupied me until I met my father a few days later. This was the first time he'd seen me since I was a few months old, but we got along remarkably well from the outset. Even more wonderful was the fact that he and James really took to each other. Perhaps unusually for an Italian Catholic, I was father's only child, so he had no other grandchildren. I learned later that he had received an 'unfortunate injury' in the course of his work, so further children had been impossible.

"When I mentioned my problem, father said he'd think about what to do. I rather thought he might suggest placing James in a seminary, instead of boarding school. You know, 'give me the boy and I'll show you the man', as the Jesuits claim.

"But the next day he said to me, '*I panni sporchi, si lavano in famiglia*'." Mrs Fielding smiled at Bryce. "At the time I had no Italian, and he had to translate that for me, but you may have enough Italian – or even Latin – to work it out."

The DCI nodded, and gave a colloquial translation for his colleagues. "Don't do your dirty washing in public."

"Yes. Not very flattering to liken James to '*panni sporchi*', but the key point was that Cameron could not yet be counted as 'family'. Father outlined a scheme – which you have guessed. James would 'die' in an accident, and as far as anyone in England was concerned, he really would be dead. In fact, he would be brought up in Italy, in his grandfather's house, and inducted into his grandfather's business as he got older. We discussed this over several days – I had no Italian, by the way, but as I said, father's English was very good.

"We discussed this over several days, and I agreed to the scheme. I'd have been a fool not to. It was doubly advantageous. James wouldn't inadvertently obstruct my getting together with Cameron, and he would be removed from England – where he'd already been in enough trouble. It would avoid a problem which I anticipated would worsen as he got older.

"I realised that I had to tell Cameron about James' existence, and about his death – if we married he would certainly have heard about it in the village otherwise. However, I never registered James' death in England, so there was no inquest – things were very lax at that time. Nor was the 'accident' ever reported in the British press. Everything went smoothly.

"Desmond and I had a flat in London, which we used for occasional visits rather than going to hotels. After the decision about James, I bought another flat in the same mansion block. For the next seven or eight years, James came over with his grandfather at least twice each year, and stayed in the new flat. I went down often during those visits – as I said, Cameron avoided London like the plague and never offered to accompany me. I went out to Italy by myself at least once each year, notionally to visit my father. Cameron, fortunately, didn't only hate London, he disliked any form of travel, and never displayed the slightest interest in coming with me – although had he ever changed his mind we had a contingency plan for concealing James.

"I probably saw almost as much of James as I would have done if he'd stayed in boarding school. When they weren't in London, I was in regular contact by letter. Cameron knew my father was Italian – we'd made some excuse as to why he couldn't attend our wedding – so the arrival of letters from Italy passed unremarked.

"Father died in 1938. For various reasons, James couldn't stay in Italy, so he returned to England to live in the flat. He still legally existed in this country, and indeed had obtained a British passport without any problem. In due course he joined the army. That was not a success, and it has to be said that James's morals are such that he would rather earn something illegally than legally if the former were even marginally easier. I increased his allowance, but that would make little difference to James' attitude.

"I don't know if you have children, Chief Inspector, but I can tell you that a parent – certainly a mother – can't stop loving her child, whatever he may be like." She smiled wanly. "Now let's come to the present.

"Mr Waring strongly disapproves of my saying this, but I make it clear to you now that I initiated all this. James simply followed my suggestions, and none of this is his fault. The blame is all mine." She raised her hand in a 'stop' signal as the Solicitor took a noisy intake of breath. "Yes, and for the reporter too. When I heard that the man was asking questions, I told James to finish him off as well. I shall plead guilty to the charges you will no doubt be putting to me shortly."

Silence followed this speech.

"Very well," said the DCI. "Perhaps you'll

make a statement to that effect?"

Waring spoke for the first time since the introductions.

"My client has already dictated a short statement, Chief Inspector. I have it here. As she says, I strongly advised her against making it, but have been overruled." He produced a single sheet of paper, and looked interrogatively at Mrs Fielding, who nodded firmly. With an almost despairing sigh, the Solicitor passed it to the DCI.

Bryce and Catchpole read the handwritten sheet together. Looking up again, the DCI said:

"That seems to cover the necessary points. Perhaps you would sign it now, Mrs Fielding?"

Bryce offered his own pen. Without hesitation Mrs Fielding wrote her full name and added her signature in a quick flourish, underscoring it twice. Waring looked as though he was about to cry.

"Thank you," continued Bryce. "Now, it's late, and the car bringing your son from London has not yet arrived. We'll conclude this interview, and talk to him in the morning."

"Just one question, Chief Inspector. Who told you that I had a son?"

"Nobody in the village had mentioned your son, Mrs Fielding. Indirectly, you told us yourself. I saw the gravestone you erected for your first husband, on which James was mentioned."

"I see. I don't know for sure, but the journalist may have spotted the same thing. It was when I heard he'd been looking in the parish register that I felt he had to be stopped."

The four officers silently listened to this the calm admission that she had ordered the second killing. Waring seemed to have given up on the sighing, and was now squeezing his eyelids tight and grimacing, as though he was in acute pain.

"So you didn't know for sure that he'd found anything?" asked the DCI. "He might have just been doing a bit of genealogy research, into his own family, perhaps. I came across a couple of Cunninghams in the register I looked at; and a gravestone in the churchyard."

"An irrelevant hypothesis as far as I am concerned. It was a risk I couldn't afford to take – and didn't take!

"You may not know – I didn't realise this myself until after George was shot – but Cunningham had originally come to Ashton to investigate George's own actions. I think he had probably heard rumours about the matters with the Redfern estate, and thought a scandal involving an Ipswich solicitor would be newsworthy. Then George died, and he began to cast his net wider – I believe that's when he first heard about my own troubles."

"I see," said Catchpole. "What I don't see is why you decided to have Wilcox killed. Why not get your revenge through legal channels? You could have sued him; even had him charged with a criminal offence – the adverse publicity and disgrace would surely have been punishment enough for him?"

"Not to my mind, Inspector. The fact that I had been weak enough to give him the opportunity to do what he did would have been just as humiliating for me. Then there was the unforgivable way that he trifled with my affections." A smile of pure satisfaction spread across Mrs Fielding's face. "He had to be dealt with properly."

"You sound more like a member of the *Mafia* than an Englishwoman," said Bryce.

The satisfied smile now became infused with arrogance. "I thought you might have worked this out, Chief Inspector. My father was a ranking member of the *Camorra* – my tragic little milksop of an English mother left him when she found out. She brought me to England when I was very young, and steeped me in her family's way of doing things.

"So you see, *retribuzione* is in my blood. And. although James inherited his fair hair and blue eyes from his father, I'm glad that he too carries the same trait."

There was a flippancy in this last remark which chilled Bryce. He felt nothing but contempt for the woman before him, whose justification for the foulest of crimes was attributed so casually and so completely to an accident of birth. He responded with uncharacteristic vehemence and the coldest of smiles. "British justice has an element of retribution in it too, Mrs Fielding. Before long, you'll be experiencing it.

"The Inspector will charge you with one offence now, although there may be at least one further matter later."

Catchpole stood to lay the charge of being an accessory before the fact in the murder of George Wilcox. "You'll be held here overnight," he continued, "and will appear before a magistrate in the morning."

"I understand," replied Mrs Fielding. "When will I be able to see James?"

"Not before we've talked to him; and probably not even then," replied Catchpole, to Bryce's approval.

"I see. Well, I'll pay for Mr Waring here to represent him, tonight or whenever you get him here. I'll also fund his representation in court, and since I shall claim that he's clearly mentally unfit – perhaps even unfit to plead – I'll pay for expert medical opinions too."

"Very well," replied the DCI, "it's your money, and your choice. The only thing for which I can't blame you is sticking by your son.

"I should really have homed in on you sooner, Mrs Fielding. Those pictures in your house. When I said a scene seemed familiar, you said they were all Welsh scenes. I felt sure they were all painted in Italy. I should have followed up on that."

Christina Fielding threw back her head and laughed. "Yes, I thought you didn't believe me, but quite unnecessarily I wanted to avoid any suggestion of Italy. How clever of you to recognise the pre-war paintings of Anzio – I suppose you were there in 1944?"

Bryce nodded wordlessly. Not wishing to discuss his war service with the woman, he addressed her Solicitor instead.

"Presumably, in view of Mrs Fielding's indication of plea, you're happy there is no conflict of interest, Mr Waring?"

"Happy isn't the word I'd use in the circumstances, Chief Inspector, but I agree there won't be any conflict. No question of a cut-throat defence."

"No. Well, Mrs Fielding, I have to say that I don't fancy your son's chances if his defence team tries to press any sort of insanity plea. As far as the M'Naghten Rules are concerned, it seems to me that he certainly knew exactly what he was doing in twice organising a hitman; and he also knew that what he was doing was wrong. And that's without his shooting of the gunman, and covering it up disguised as a soldier."

"He was a soldier," expostulated the woman.

"Yes, but no longer entitled to wear the uniform. Also it seems he has subsequently disposed of both that and the pistol – another indication that he knew what he did was wrong."

Mrs Fielding made no response.

Bryce looked across to Catchpole and nodded.

"Lock her up again, Jephson," instructed the Inspector. "I assume you'll come back in the morning to speak to Johnson, Mr Waring – we won't be talking to him tonight."

Waring nodded, gathered up his papers, and followed Jephson out of the room.

Bryce stretched his arms above his head and yawned. "Straight to the Bull for us, Haig, I think, and no doubt everyone else wants to get home, too."

Catchpole nodded. "I'll tell the desk man to book your two DCs into a hotel – they won't be fit to drive back to London tonight. We'll get them in the Bull if there are any vacancies."

"Much appreciated; thank you," said Bryce, as he and Haig reached for their hats and coats.

CHAPTER 17

The following morning, Haig was down to breakfast first, and almost collided with Kittow and Barker at the dining room door.

"Didn't expect to be put up overnight, Sarge," said Kittow. "Very kind of Suffolk, because we didn't really fancy another three-hour journey in the dark."

As the men were taking their seats for breakfast, the DCI joined them to a chorus of 'good mornings'.

"I was just saying, sir, we're grateful for the stopover. We didn't arrive until after eleven o'clock, and thought we'd have to drive back in the dark. No overnight things, but the hotel didn't seem to mind."

"What was the journey like?"

"Pretty awful, really," replied Kittow. "A lot of traffic leaving London, followed by a diversion which took us miles around Chelmsford. Then to top it all we got lost coming through Ipswich." He glanced significantly at Barker, who looked embarrassed."

A waitress took their breakfast orders. When she had gone, the DCI continued:

"There's nobody within earshot if we speak quietly. Tell us about the arrest, and what Johnson has said."

"We went to Islington," said Kittow. "The local DDI, Mr Pettit, came himself. He brought two local DCs, so there were five of us. He and one of his DCs came armed. Mr Pettit sent one of his men round the back, told me to wait across the road with the other, and then he and Barker knocked on the door."

Barker took up the tale. "Johnson wasn't in, so we forced the door and went in. Mr Pettit sent me out with instructions for Kittow and the two round the back. The armed DC was to wait with Kittow, keep the door under observation, and take the target if he appeared. The rest of us started to search – there were two bedrooms and two living rooms – quite a decent place."

Kittow resumed.

"We'd seen a picture from Records, so we knew who to watch for. There was a handy tea shop almost opposite, and we hadn't been there more than half an hour when we saw the man coming along. We nipped out sharpish, and grabbed him just as he was putting his key in the street door to the mansion block. Neither of us even drew our pistols. Took him inside."

Barker took up the narrative again.

"Before they brought Johnson in, we'd found

some letters tucked inside a book. They were all on headed paper, from Strickland House, Ashton. Mr Pettit told me to take those and keep them out of Johnson's sight if he came in. The letters are in the nick here now, sir.

"When Johnson came in handcuffed to Kittow, Mr Pettit arrested and cautioned him. Johnson didn't speak, even when he was asked a couple of direct questions. He looked totally shocked.

"We went over the whole place. There was no army uniform, and no gun, in Johnson's rooms or anywhere, sir. So when we'd been over every inch, Mr Pettit told us to take Johnson away. We handcuffed him to a chain attached to the car door."

"We were in the car with him for three hours or so, and he never said one word all that time." finished Kittow.

A waitress arrived with beverages, and few seconds later another brought the kippers which Bryce and Haig had ordered, and the bacon and eggs selected by Kittow and Barker. There followed five minutes of silence as the men enjoyed their meals.

"I'm sorry to have to send you straight back," said Bryce to the DCs, "it would've been good experience for you to observe Johnson's interview. But it's really a Suffolk case, and of course their two local officers must sit in. Yesterday there were four of us in with the mother and her solicitor, and that was too many. We can't possibly get eight in that room!"

"From what we've heard, it may be that the Johnson interview is short and silent," laughed Haig.

***

Back at the police station, the junior Yard detectives drove off, and Bryce and Haig went inside. The desk man reported that Mr Waring was now with his new client. Inspector Catchpole had not yet arrived – Sergeant Jephson had come in earlier, but had since left on another case.

Bryce told the officer to ask the lawyer to say when he and his client were ready for interview.

In the office, the DCI picked up the folder left by Kittow and Barker. He shook out four letters. Each, as Barker had said, was on headed paper, and opened with 'My Dearest James'.

Bryce read them in chronological order, passing each to Haig as soon as he finished it. Neither man spoke as they read.

When Haig handed back the last letter, the DCI returned them all to the folder. He leaned back in his chair and looked at his Sergeant.

"Observations?"

"Well, sir, even if Mrs F hadn't admitted what she did, these letters would be enough to convict her anyway.

"But taking the correspondence between them as a whole, I'd say the exchange showed two people discussing quite rationally how to eliminate two separate victims. She asked him to do both killings, yes – but his responses seem to show a very clear understanding not only about how to arrange them but also how to get away with them. And that means he knew he was doing wrong. The only argument in favour of insanity is the fact that they were both stupid enough to put their plans in writing – and then to retain the letters."

Bryce agreed. "Absolutely. That's the case in a nutshell."

Inspector Catchpole arrived, and after the usual greetings, the DCI passed the letters over to the Suffolk man. After reading them, he looked up and spoke. As he finished, both Yard officers started to laugh. Catchpole looked at them enquiringly.

"We're laughing because what you've just said is almost word for word what Sergeant Haig said a few minutes ago – it's uncanny!

"Anyway, we're all satisfied about the significance of the correspondence. Hopefully, Waring won't keep us waiting too long.

"By the way, Catchpole, are you keeping your boss informed? I haven't attempted to do that, and I haven't even started to write my report."

"Yes, sir, I've been in daily contact. I spoke to the Superintendent yesterday afternoon, and the Chief Constable himself called me when I was at breakfast this morning. He'd never done anything like that before. My landlady took the call, and initially thought it was one of my colleagues playing a joke. The CC thought it was quite funny, fortunately."

The Met officers grinned. "Well, I've got a call to make now that I wish wasn't necessary," said Bryce, picking up the telephone. He asked to be connected to the City police station in Bishopsgate, and waited until he got through to DI Playford.

"I'd better give you an early warning, Inspector. I'm afraid your 'justifiable homicide' at Liverpool Street was nothing of the kind. Just plain, cold-blooded murder, as it turns out."

He explained the situation. The unfortunate Playford quickly realised that he was not going to emerge from the investigation smelling of roses.

"Oh, dear Lord – and I even gave him back his gun!"

"Well, it could have been far worse; fortunately he wasn't carrying it when he was arrested, and so couldn't make use of it again.

"Anyway, this will hit the press soon – maybe the evening papers today, because I imagine Suffolk will be putting out a statement shortly.

"It's up to you, Playford, but I suggest you inform your boss before he hears it from other sources. Better update the Coroner, too.

"It won't be much consolation to you, but if I'd been in your shoes, with the information you had that night, I'd have come to exactly the same conclusion you did, and done precisely the same. You can quote me to Sir Hugh if you wish!"

"Thanks, sir; I appreciate that. Not sure it'll stop my Super from roasting me alive, but perhaps it'll mean I'm only demoted to sergeant rather than all the way back down to constable!"

Ending the call, Bryce asked for another line, as there was still no sign of Lucas Waring. He contacted Islington, and passed on his thanks to DDI Pettit, an old acquaintance. He learned that enquiries were being made about where the missing pistol and uniform might have gone. Also about how Johnson learned about Sullivan's existence. For the purposes of the prosecution, the relationship between the two men wasn't significant – nothing would turn on it in court. However, establishing links might provide valuable information about criminal networks in London and beyond.

Putting the telephone down again, Bryce was about to speak when there was knock on the door. A constable poked his head into the room, and announced that Mr Waring and his client were ready.

"Bring them along at once," instructed Catchpole. He asked the DCI if coffee was in order, and on receiving a 'yes' told the constable to arrange this for five people.

CHAPTER 18

Waring came into the room. If anything, he looked even more unhappy than he had the previous evening. He was followed by James Johnson, handcuffed to the Desk Sergeant. Bringing up the rear was a Constable with a tray.

"Sit him down the other side of the table, Sergeant, and take off the cuffs," said Catchpole. "Then leave him with us – he can't get out of here with the three of us in the way."

Waring sat beside his client, with Bryce and Catchpole opposite. Sergeant Haig positioned his chair in front of the door as soon as the other two officers had gone.

None of those in the room had seen Johnson before, and they stared at him with interest. Tall and handsome he was casually but expensively dressed, and looked every inch like a film hero – the antithesis of the cinematic stereotype of a killer. He was, as they knew, in his late twenties, and appeared perfectly normal. After being picked up in London, driven to Suffolk, and passing a night in the cells, his clothing was inevitably a little crumpled and he was in need of a shave. However, he had managed to comb a neat parting in his fair hair, and despite the stubble on his chin still somehow managed to look eminently presentable.

Inspector Catchpole identified himself, and introduced the Yard detectives.

"I understand your client was cautioned on arrest yesterday, Mr Waring," he continued, "but I'll repeat it now to be certain."

Having done that, Catchpole looked at the DCI to take over.

"You know why we're here, Mr Johnson," said Bryce. "You presumably also know that your mother is here as well. She spoke to us at length yesterday, as no doubt Mr Waring has explained. Now it's your turn."

"My Solicitor here advises me to say nothing," said Johnson.

"That was indeed my policy yesterday, when I was arrested. However, I've since learned that my mother is seeking to take the blame. I cannot sit by and permit you to believe that. It's totally wrong. I was the initiator. I understand that my mother chose to ignore Mr Waring's advice yesterday, and I agree with him that she was foolish to do so. However, my situation is different, and with all respect to Mr Waring I shall also disregard him. Ask me what you will.

"Incidentally, in my several visits to Met police stations, I've never been offered refreshments – and this is rather better coffee than one might expect in a rural station, so it's doubly appreciated."

Bryce ignored this remark, while mentally noting how similar Johnson was to his mother in the matter of making irrelevant small talk.

"Tell us first about George Wilcox," said the DCI. "Did you know him?"

"I'd met him years before. He moved to Ashton when I was seven or eight years old. I was already away at boarding school, so I only saw him in the holidays. He and his wife came to our house quite often to play bridge with my parents. He was always good to me – gave me the odd half-crown.

"As you know, I left the country. I hadn't seen or heard of the man for twenty or so years, until mother told me what he'd done. I decided to kill him for that."

Sergeant Haig, mug in hand, delayed taking a swallow of his coffee, so astonished was he at Johnson's *sang-froid*. The man's manner and tone were both consistent with a conversation about the weather, or the price of potatoes.

"When did you learn that your grandfather was a member of the *Camorra*?" asked Bryce.

"It probably didn't dawn on me until I'd lived with him for a year or two. To start with, you see, everything was so different for me – and I didn't speak the language. In fact grandfather was the only person I could speak to for months, and he never said anything about what he did. But after a couple of years I began to realise – and frankly I found it exciting. Gradually, grandfather drew me more into his business. When I was sixteen, he explained that one day I'd be expected to take his place in the organisation.

"Why did you return to England, then?" asked Catchpole.

"That was unplanned. Everything was fine while the old man was alive, and in control of his men. But when he died there was something of a revolt. A lot of jealousy suddenly came out into the open. It was said, by a powerful cabal, that because I was only a half-blood member it would be unsafe to trust me. The Italians have a saying about oxen and wives – they should be chosen from your own region. Grandfather's men felt the same about their next *capo*. I saw the writing on the wall, and left Italy before I got taken out!"

"Interesting," said Bryce. "So you made a decision, but how did you know where to find a professional hitman in London?"

"Initially I considered doing the job myself. Speaking frankly, I'd helped in a few similar actions during the year or so before grandfather died. However, I decided it would be safer to use a professional. I asked a few people I knew. It wasn't hard to get a name – Abe Dean – but it was very difficult to make contact. He operated through two intermediaries – sort of cut-outs. I'll give you their names later – I know that at least one was in on the scheme to blackmail me, so I'm not going to shield them."

"Did you meet Dean eventually?"

"No, never did. Not until Liverpool Street – and we hardly had a conversation there!"

"Let's come back to that. So you agreed a fee with him – or with his agents – for killing Wilcox?"

"With the second agent, yes – seven hundred and fifty pounds. Payable in advance. I provided the details of where Wilcox lived, and the lie of the land. Even suggested where Dean could park out of sight.

"That went ahead, and as far as I know nobody saw either Dean or his car."

"Apart from Mr Allen," interjected Catchpole.

"Yes – so I gathered. That was unfortunate. I could hardly blame Dean for getting rid of a witness, but I had no grudge against Allen. I'd also known him for a time years ago, and he too was decent to me."

Johnson's words conveyed regret, but his tone and manner spoke of a cold indifference to Allen's fate.

"But apart from that, all had gone well. Then I learned that some newspaper hack was sniffing around. Mother thought he might have discovered my existence. I decided to spend another seven hundred and fifty pounds. Knowing the form now, I went via the agents again, agreed terms, and fixed the venue and time. Very short notice. I telephoned the reporter to set him up. He was so gullible. Told him I had evidence, but I didn't want to talk to the police."

"Come back to the blackmail, now," said Bryce.

"Yes. I had agreed the fee for the journalist, but hadn't actually paid it because the notice was so short. As a previous client, apparently my credit was good. However, only hours later, I got a message to say that the job would now cost twelve hundred. Take it or leave it – and it was made clear that if I didn't agree not only would the second hit not take place, but you lot would be tipped off anonymously about my involvement with Wilcox."

Johnson gave a brittle laugh. "I was never going to let that happen. Also, Dean knew that I had money, and it seemed probable that he'd have bled me for evermore. Whether he tried to blackmail other clients as well, I don't know.

"I didn't have much time to plan. I could probably never find Dean – I didn't even know what he looked like. My only hope was to get him that night when I knew exactly where he would be.

"So I told the agent I agreed to the new terms. I cleaned my old Colt automatic, pressed my old uniform, and went to Liverpool Street.

"Until the last minute, I hadn't decided whether to present myself as a public-spirited soldier, and bluff it out, or to run for it, relying on the fact that nobody would have recognised me. In fact I didn't decide until after I'd shot Dean. The very nice girl in the red coat who later came to the police station with me had been close enough to have recognised me. She seemed too pretty to kill, so my decision was made.

"Anyway, I'm familiar enough with the station. It wasn't difficult to watch where the Norwich train was coming in, and I spotted Dean for what he was, even before he pulled out his shotgun. My position up on the footbridge was perfect, and I could have cut him off whichever way he turned to leave. I came down the steps and shot him, as you know. It was a risk, of course, but everything went exactly as I'd hoped. And the nice young woman who witnessed what happened apparently helped no end by truthfully stating that Dean started to raise his gun before I fired. So I was extra glad that I hadn't shot her! And I can't fault your colleagues at the nearby police station – they were very understanding.

"Incidentally, I'd never been involved with the City of London police, so I knew that the chance of one of their officers recognising me was nil. That might have been different if I'd had to do the job in Paddington, or Euston."

"The City officer you met may now face a lot of tricky questions following that 'understanding'," said the DCI, "although I'd have treated you the same, as I've told him. You acted out the scene very well.

"I assume your mother paid for the first job, and would have funded the second?"

Johnson hesitated, realising the significance

of this question. "No, Chief Inspector. I'm not poor – I make a reasonable income from various illegal sources, and mother makes me a handsome allowance on top of the money grandfather gave her while he was alive."

"So if we find that your mother transferred seven hundred and fifty pounds to you a day or so before Wilcox was killed, what would you say to that?"

"Merely a coincidence. She often gave me lump sums as well as the regular allowance."

"We'll see what the jury thinks about that. Will you tell us something of your other enterprises?"

"No, Chief Inspector. You're going to get me hanged, so those other enterprises will die with me. But apart from Dean's agents, I have nothing against those who worked with me, so I'm not giving you their details."

"What did you do with the pistol and uniform?"

"There was a bomb site near me which was being cleared, and they were having the usual big bonfire. I chucked the uniform on that. The Colt had value. So I sold it – the buyer was obviously going to erase all the serial numbers anyway, and I watched him do that to make sure the thing could never be traced back to me."

"So when you shot Dean, the serial number was still there? That was an incredible risk – the police might well have checked on it."

"True. But I correctly gambled that they wouldn't. I presented myself as a jolly decent sort of chap." Johnson threw back his head and laughed. "An upstanding and courageous type who doesn't attract suspicion or even close scrutiny – and of course I didn't. The Inspector accommodated my every wish – even suggesting how my name could be kept out of the matter." He laughed again at the recollection.

"Perhaps an even bigger risk was that they'd ask, purely as a formality, to see my ID. I no longer had army papers – all I could show was a civilian ID card. And as that was perfectly genuine, it was in my real name. So I didn't dare to give a false name at the police station. Actually, if they'd asked it would have looked very odd for a soldier to be carrying civvy ID. But again, they took my uniform at face value, and checked nothing – more fool them! I shall be sorry if the Inspector gets into trouble though – he was perfectly pleasant to me."

Much of what Johnson was saying tied in with the DCI's own theories about how the ex-soldier had covered his tracks, but not everything had been explained, and he was still curious.

"You told him that you were about to leave the army, presumably so the police didn't try to contact you in Colchester. How did you plan to deal with the next step – the inquest on Dean?"

"To be honest, I hadn't decided. I promised the police I'd give them my new address in a few days. It was really a question of assessing the new risk – which was perhaps even greater than the one in Liverpool Street. If I gave them my real address, could I maintain the bluff in court when called to give evidence? The inquest would inevitably attract a lot of attention. I guessed it wouldn't be hard to persuade the Coroner to keep my name secret, and the Inspector had even suggested as much. But someone from the Press might take a photograph outside the court. Very unlikely that anyone in Ashton would recognise me after all these years, even in the improbable event of the local paper covering the inquest. But some Met police officer, who knew me as a common criminal rather than as a respectable army officer, might spot the picture and ask awkward questions. Or someone in the Norfolks might be suspicious.

"The alternative solution was to acquire false papers – not difficult – and then to disappear. However, that would inevitably mean that questions would be asked about my identity – and that would almost certainly lead to my mother.

"I was veering towards a sort of compromise. I had almost decided to give the police an accommodation address, where I could be contacted to be informed about the inquest, but through which I could never be traced again. If there was a hue and cry later, I could either retreat to mother's flat, or disappear to another city under a new name.

"Actually, I thought the odds were still well in my favour if I continued with the bluff. I'd go to court, give my evidence, and then hurry away as soon as possible, keeping my head down. We'll never know now whether I'd have been successful."

Johnson spread his hands. "There you have it; everything I did."

"Let's get a statement from you, then," said Bryce. "It can be quite simple, but include the details of Dean's 'agents' if you will."

Leaning towards his client, the Solicitor again urged caution. "I have to advise you again not to do that. You've already said far more than is wise."

Johnson scoffed unpleasantly. "You still don't seem to understand. I'm taking full responsibility for the deaths of Wilcox and the reporter. In front of these officers, under caution, I've already said enough to convict me. Appending my signature to a written statement saying the same thing doesn't make my position any worse."

Waring, his second client also seeming hell-bent on running towards the gallows, sat back in resignation and took an enormous swallow of his now lukewarm coffee, looking as if he would have preferred something substantially stronger.

"I'll write it myself, gentlemen, if you let me have some paper," suggested Johnson.

Catchpole pushed a foolscap pad across the table,

Johnson produced a fountain pen from his jacket pocket. "I'll probably need some more ink," he said. Catchpole left the room to find a bottle, and returned a minute later.

Waring and the detectives watched in complete silence as Johnson's pen flew over the paper. He barely hesitated on coming to the end of one sentence before starting the next. After four minutes, he paused to refill his pen. After another five minutes of almost continuous writing, he stopped. He read through what he had written, signed after the final sentence, and then signed again at the bottom of each of the previous sheets.

Correctly interpreting the expression on the officers' faces, he smiled wryly. "Oh yes, gentlemen – I have enough previous experience to know what I need to write in the introduction, and that I have to sign each page!"

He pushed four sheets of paper across the table to the DCI.

While Bryce was reading, Johnson spoke again:

"You'll all be thinking, 'this man had a good upbringing, for the first few years anyway; how did he go so wrong?' To be honest, I can't really understand it myself. Yes, I had a good home, and initially I was sent to good schools. Everyone I ever met treated me well – but I just wasn't a decent person myself. I fitted in with the *Camorra* far better! My one regret is that my comrades thought otherwise after grandfather died, But maybe I have a screw loose, as they say."

He turned towards the Solicitor. "Perhaps

you and counsel will be able to make something out of that, although I'm not sure that the idea of spending the rest of my days in Broadmoor is attractive."

The DCI finished reading, and passed the statement to Catchpole, remarking, "Refreshingly comprehensive."

The DI passed each sheet to Haig as he finished reading it. There was another short silence.

"Well, Mr Johnson," said Bryce when the Sergeant reached the last page, "we can get on with charging you. Inspector?"

"James Johnson, I charge you with the murder of Alvin Sullivan, also known as Abe Dean, contrary to Common Law. I also charge you with being an accessory before the fact in the murders of George Wilcox and Marcus Cunningham, contrary to the Offences Against The Person Act.

"No doubt your Solicitor will explain what happens next. Do you want to talk to your client further, Mr Waring? If so I'll have him taken to the interview room."

Waring indicated that he did wish to converse further. Catchpole went to the door and bellowed along the corridor for someone to come.

When Johnson had been removed, Waring, who had also stood up, hesitated.

Anticipating the Solicitor's question, Catchpole said, "We don't have any facilities here for duplicating the statement. And, of course, there's the correspondence between your clients, which you've heard about but haven't yet seen. If it's okay with you, I'll get someone to make typewritten transcripts of everything, and get them to you tomorrow."

"Yes, thank you, Inspector. It's not that which is most troubling to me. I have two clients, both facing capital charges, and both refusing my advice. I can't help feeling impotent – might as well not have been here." Waring accompanied this self-deprecating comment with a regretful shrug, and turned to look directly at Bryce.

"After you came to see my senior partner, Chief Inspector, he made some enquiries about you and discovered that you're a barrister. Off the record, what are my clients' chances?"

Bryce invited the lawyer to sit down again.

"I know no more than you. But if you want my opinion, in both cases I'd say neither has any chance of acquittal. The Crown will have to make a few decisions about both your clients, of course.

"I'm guessing, but I'd expect Mrs Fielding to be indicted for the Wilcox matter only – the Cunningham matter would then lie on the table. Following her admission, she seems likely to plead guilty. But in a capital matter the judge will still require evidence, and regardless of what her son says, the correspondence – and evidence of payment – is quite enough to show her direct involvement. End of story.

"Again, it's a guess, but in Johnson's case I

think the prosecution will only go ahead with the murder of Sullivan. In the very unlikely event of that failing, there are the two accessory matters to fall back on.

"There's a certain irony in his murder charge. I simply don't believe that a professional assassin would involve himself in blackmail. Word would spread, and he'd get no more work. I suspect, but we may never know, that one of the agents was the blackmailer, and that Sullivan was completely ignorant about it. If so, Johnson had no need to shoot him. If he hadn't decided to kill the killer, I doubt if we'd have ever solved the case. Incidentally, I doubt if the threat to involve us would have materialised either – far too risky for the blackmailer, and I can't think Sullivan would have been pleased to have police enquiries getting near his door.

"Anyway, I think the Crown may request separate trials, even though some evidence will be duplicated. But I could be wrong. Your barrister might argue that they should be dealt with together. I shouldn't like to say which would be preferable for your clients.

"But I would say this: you remarked earlier that there was no conflict – no question of a cut-throat defence. However, it seems to me that there may well be a conflict of the opposite kind – each of your clients saying the other is innocent. Perhaps an unprecedented situation! However, what each of them wrote in their letters may scupper that position for both of them."

Waring nodded unhappily. "I see what you mean. What a mess."

The DCI continued. "You heard what I said to Mrs Fielding about her son's chances of invoking the M'Naghten Rules. Nothing whatsoever has emerged from the interview with him to alter my opinion – if anything, Johnson has reinforced my view that he knew exactly what he was doing, and that he knew perfectly well that it was wrong."

Waring gave another heavy sigh. "I can't argue with that here, Chief Inspector, although no doubt we'll be doing so at trial. But I have to admit that after their admissions it does seem probable that mother and son will be hanged together. I can't think of a precedent for that."

"Not together, Mr Waring, although not far apart. He'll be in Pentonville, and she'll be in Holloway.

"One thing that will interest me at trial," remarked Catchpole, "is if Mrs Fielding mentions her father and his *Camorra* allegiance."

"I'm not sure whether that would help either her or her son, Inspector," replied Waring. "Rather the reverse, probably, whatever she might think now. Anyway, perhaps the Crown will introduce it. We'll see." He stood up, shook hands with each of the three policemen, and left.

"We'll make tracks as well," said Bryce to Catchpole, "and leave you and your local prosecuting solicitor to decide about where to send these two. As I said earlier, if Johnson is indicted for the Sullivan murder, he'll need to be taken to London quite soon. If they are tried separately, his mother will probably be dealt with at the Suffolk Assizes, since her actions and the Wilcox murder occurred here."

"Well, I'll get them both in front of the Woodbridge magistrates in the morning. I'll talk to our solicitor as soon as possible, and see what he says. It'll be inconvenient in any case – Ipswich hasn't had a prison since the nineteen-twenties, so they'll probably both have to be remanded to London."

"Good luck with it all anyway," smiled the DCI. "I'll let you have my written report in a day or so. We'll collect our gear from the hotel now, and disappear. Look forward to seeing you at the Felixstowe trial in a few weeks."

Catchpole shook hands with both Yard officers. "I need hardly say I'm very grateful, just like last time," he said. "Working with you is certainly an education!"

"Hear, hear," said Haig.

"Oh come on, Catchpole," retorted Bryce. "This was solved by pure accident – there was no detective work involved."

Both Catchpole and Haig shook their heads.

****

BOOKS IN THIS SERIES

Chief Inspector Bryce Murder Mysteries

The Bedroom Window Murder

It is 1949. Sir Francis Sherwood – WW1 hero, landowner, magistrate – is shot dead while standing at an open bedroom window in his country house. A rifle is found in the grounds.

The county police seek help from Scotland Yard.

Detective Chief Inspector Bryce and Detective Sergeant Haig are assigned to the case. The first difficulty for the Yard men is that nobody with even a mild dislike of Sherwood can be found.

But before that problem can be resolved, others arise…

The Courthouse Murder

In July 1949, an unpopular and deeply unpleasant man is stabbed in the courthouse of an English city. As the murder has been committed in a room to which the general public doesn't have access, it seems probable that the culprit is someone involved with the business of the courts.

Suspects include a number of lawyers, police officers, and magistrates.

For various reasons, the local Chief Constable decides to ask Scotland Yard to investigate the murder.

Chief Inspector Philip Bryce and Sergeant Alex Haig are assigned to the case.

Theirs is a recent partnership, but the two men worked well together in another murder case a few weeks before. (See 'The Bedroom Window Murder'.)

The Felixstowe Murder

In August 1949, Detective Chief Inspector Bryce and his new bride are holidaying in the East Anglian seaside resort of Felixstowe.

During afternoon tea in the Palm Court of their hotel, a man dies at a nearby table.

Reluctant to get directly involved, Bryce nevertheless agrees to help the inexperienced local police inspector get to grips with his first murder case, turning his own honeymoon into a 'busman's holiday'.

Multiples Of Murder

Three more cases for Philip Bryce. The first two are set in 1949, and follow on from The Bedroom Window Murder, The Courthouse Murder, and The Felixstowe Murder.
The third goes back to 1946, when Bryce – not long back in the police after his army service – was a mere Detective Inspector, based in Whitechapel rather than Scotland Yard.

1. In the office kitchen of a small advertising agency in London, a man falls to the floor, dead. Initially, it is believed that he had some sort of heart attack, but it soon becomes clear that he had received a fatal electric shock. A faulty kettle is then blamed. But evidence emerges showing that this was not an accident. Chief Inspector Bryce is assigned to the case.

2. Just before opening time, a body is found in the larger pool at the huge public baths in St

Marylebone. The man has been shot, presumably the previous evening. It is DCI Bryce's task, aided by Detective Sergeant Haig and others, to discover the identity of the victim, why he was killed, and who shot him.

3. For a few months in 1946, a traditional London bus was modified in an experiment to allow passengers to 'Pay-As-You-Board'. Doors were fitted, instead of having the usual open platform. The stairs rose from inside the saloon rather than directly from the platform. On the upper deck, a man is found stabbed to death. None of the passengers can shed any light on the murder, yet the design of this bus meant that no-one could have jumped off the bus unnoticed – one of them must be the murderer. Inspector Bryce, together with colleagues from Leman Street police station, solves one of his earlier cases.

Death At Mistram Manor

In September 1949, a wake is being held at a manor house in Oxfordshire, following the burial of the chatelaine. Over a hundred mourners are present.

Within an hour, the clergyman who conducted the funeral service is taken ill himself. The local doctor, present at the wake, provisionally diagnoses appendicitis, and calls for an ambulance. However, the priest dies soon after being admitted to hospital.

An autopsy reveals that the cause of death was strychnine poisoning.

The circumstances are such that accidental ingestion and suicide are both ruled out. The rector was murdered, and the timing means that the poison must have been taken during the wake.

The local police, faced with a lengthy list of potential suspects, ask Scotland Yard to take on the investigation, and the case is assigned to Detective Chief Inspector Bryce and two colleagues.

Although most of the mourners can easily be eliminated from the enquiry, around eight of them cannot. The experienced London officers have to sift through a number of initially-promising indications, before finally being able to identify the killer.

Machinations Of A Murderer

There are at least two reasons why Robin Whitaker wants to eliminate his wife, Dulcie. He is not allowed to drink any alcohol, nor to gamble.

Dulcie controls his life to an extent that he finds

intolerable. But she is also wealthy, so merely leaving her is not an acceptable option.

In most circumstances Dr Whitaker thinks and acts like the very intelligent and highly-educated man he is. However, he has somehow convinced himself that the action of killing his wife is justified. He is also certain that his innate brainpower will give him a significant edge over any police detectives, and allow him to outwit them with ease.

What are his thoughts? How does he make his decisions? What does he do?

Will he get away with murder?

Suspicions Of A Parlourmaid And The Norfolk Railway Murders

Two more cases for Philip Bryce.

1 An affluent elderly lady dies. The death certificate cites 'natural causes', but the servants are uncomfortable.

A parlourmaid decides to go to New Scotland Yard, and talk to someone there. She is fortunate, because Detective Sergeant Haig happens to pass through the foyer while she is explaining. The busy desk officer intercepts him, and asks to him to listen to the maid's story.

Haig listens politely, but is ready to dismiss the story as tittle-tattle, when he hears one thing which makes him take notice. He goes to report to his boss, DCI Bryce, who also finds the point of interest, and goes downstairs to speak to the maid himself.

The full might of the Metropolitan Police is then focussed on the matter – and a post mortem examination reveals that the lady was indeed poisoned.

Where did the poison come from? How was it administered? Who did it, and why? In the leafy South London suburb of Dulwich Village, Bryce and Haig investigate the happenings, and sort out who is innocent, and who is guilty.

2. DCI Bryce is sent to Norfolk, where two solicitors have been killed. There are obvious connections between the crimes. First, both men were partners in the same firm. But also, both appeared to have been killed while travelling on local railway trains, and the bodies then thrown off. Over the whole existence of railways in Britain, the number of such cases could be counted on the fingers of one hand. So one such case would have been rare enough, but for there to be two – on different trains and a few days apart – was almost unbelievable.

However, shortly before these two men were found, a third body was discovered. This victim didn't seem to have any connection to the firm of solicitors – but he too was found beside a railway track.

A temporary absence of CID officers in King's Lynn causes the Chief Constable to ask Scotland Yard to take the case. DCI Bryce and two of his officers travel to West Norfolk, where they find a local Detective Constable eager to help.

Which of the three victims was the real target, and which murders were either dry runs or red herrings?

Printed in Great Britain
by Amazon